RANSOM
of the
Golden Bridge

The *unthinkable* becomes a matter of daily conversation with these crooks. 'Hyenas' is what the breezy blonde calls her co-conspirators.

Persons of highest authority in the United States are believably involved with political activists, con men, FBI agents, and bureaucrats, all of whom combine to tell this story of the Golden Gate Bridge.

While people should be celebrating the bridge's fifty years of service, the *unthinkable* is being planned.

"A dandy caper story . . ." Herb Caen, San Francisco Chronicle

of the
GOLDEN
BRIDGE

PROCTOR JONES
San Francisco

PUBLISHER'S NOTE

The characters in this book are all fictitious. The events are all imagined. The technical matters mentioned have no foundation in practice or experience. Indeed, there was a Joseph B. Strauss, a Bailey Willis, and Presidents Hoover and Truman. To my certain knowledge, none of them was familiar with what is related here.

Published by Proctor Jones Publishing Company, San Francisco, CA.

Designed by Ed Gross, Mill Valley, CA. Back cover photograph by Proctor Jones, Jr. Production by George Waters, Menlo Park, CA.

Library of Congress No. 83–080825

ISBN 0–9608860–2–8

First Printing April, 1983.

Second Printing September, 1990

DEDICATION

This story is dedicated to A. P. Giannini who, with $4 million, bridged the Gate, thereby making this story possible.

It is also dedicated to the 300,000 daily users of the Bridge to whom the possibilities of such a tale must already have occurred.

CHAPTER ONE

Radio blaring hot rock, the sleek black car slowly made its way across a misty Golden Gate.

The dark eyed driver, George Mortelli, chewing a wad of gum, drove as though in a trance. "Yeah," he thought. "It can be done."

Once across, he took a sharp right into the observation parking lot facing San Francisco. He looked right straight down the tarmac of the Golden Gate Bridge. Moving along, he found a parking space. He pulled in and closed the windows. He jumped from the car and locked it. His eyes never seemed to leave the steel girders of the span. He left the car and moved off to the right, following a little path which permitted a closer view of the engineering marvel.

Some young kids yelled past him, diverting him for just an instant.

"Yes," he said to himself, "it can be done."

He was a very slight man with an intent face. No father would be happy to have his daughter with this fellow on the porch swing. If he were studied for a moment or two, it became obvious that he was not a shifty type, which was disappointing. The car, the radio, the guy's build spelled 'shifty.' He was sure of himself. You picked this up on the second glance, just as you were making the decision about the porch swing.

1

He took a small camera from his pocket and made a quick photograph in a spot no artist would choose. He was an 'artist' all right, but his prizes were not for photographs. He made his way back up the hill. Opening the car, he took one last look at the towers.

Not one person of the 250 gathered there to look at the wind swept San Francisco skyline would be able to describe him or his car. He slipped out into the stream of happy weekenders heading for the joys of northern Marin County and waypoints. Finally, he turned off and followed a heavily-trafficked two lane road. Another turn and he was practically by himself. Houses, gas stations, stores were left behind, and he started to climb and turn onto the wooded mountain.

A complete wilderness enveloped the car, driver, chewing gum and music. The road climbed higher, then a driveway appeared to drop off to the left. Like a graceful bird, his car swerved to flow in descending curves. The drive led to a lodge in the trees. Through a window in the branches, a careful visitor could see the bridge towers fighting with the wind-driven fog. He did not look.

He stopped the car before a shed attached to the lodge. Some instrument in his car opened an overhead door and the car was devoured by a dark cavern. The shed's door closed. Taking his camera equipment from his car, he walked to a staircase leading into the lodge. He went straight to his darkroom to develop the messages his camera had collected.

The darkroom phone shrilled for attention. With his wet hand, he held the receiver. It was Reno calling. "Yes," he said quickly. Then he did not speak, but listened. Finally, he said, "Yes, Volta. It can be done."

CHAPTER TWO

On the Reno end of the line, a balding wisp of a man with the small darting eyes of a ferret put down the telephone receiver. Volta Orpath squinted out of the window. The mountain in the distance made its familiar march from the desert floor to the horizon.

He took a long yellow pencil in both hands as if to break it. Resting his elbows on the desk in front of him, he nodded his head forward and tapped his slightly-protruding teeth against the wood of the pencil. He was thinking.

Even before George had told him, he knew it could be done. That much was settled. What he had not yet decided was whether or not he wanted to do it. He was sixty-nine years old. An alert and wiry sixty-nine. He really didn't want to 'retire' just yet. One more job. One crowning escapade. One more campaign, just to show that he could still do it. Something to touch off the career of an ace con man.

He didn't need the money. He had made a very good thing out of a crooked existence.

Not having attractive features, or family, he had to depend on his brain. In the late 1920's, he worked the board in a big stock-brokerage house in New York City. His take was about twenty dollars a week. By sleeping at the YMCA, he managed to save some part of his salary, if not his soul.

3

When the great shock of 1929 came, he had a modest bundle in the bank, in a safety-deposit vault. With great foresight he wasn't trusting the bankers or anyone else. He had made a curbside study of the American investing animal and had early decided that such stupid gambling could lead only to a jump from a window, or, at least, to great disappointment.

Then he learned what happens when the bottom falls out. He waited patiently for the last cry of despair.

When the water was on its way somewhere else, he bought. He laid the foundation for modest wealth.

Orpath then worked some interesting con games with travelers in from the West. When he was finished with them, they were lucky to have carfare.

As the Thirties opened, he reached into more lucrative fields. Mail fraud. Improper insurance procedures. And once, believe it or not, a radio church's scheme that received many hard-earned Bible-belt dollars.

He wasn't the minister. He was the treasurer. The minister thought that he was managing the rake himself, but more slipped through than stuck. Religion having paid off, Orpath was on to other pastures. A kidnapped load of bullion in Australia for one thing.

Then crooked Army-supply contracts. The only people who found out how bad his merchandise was generally didn't live to complain about it. After the War, he went into the industrial secrets business. He ran into a beaten-up B-26 pilot, Elton 'Puggo' Alexander, who caught his eye during one of his capers, and they became friends. Puggo was the only 'friend' Orpath had. Together they worked the business 'secrets' racket.

Puggo could get a job anywhere as a Security Guard.

4

He looked like one. Orpath always knew the right places.

Then it became a game, peddling the stuff. The payoff was rewarding.

Puggo received a sort of salary. He always thought, in a cloudy way, that he should receive more, but he never argued with Orpath about the amount. At least, he ate.

George Mortelli had walked into Orpath's company by accident. George, being young in the con game, did not recognize Orpath as another con man; thought he was some insecure little jerk he'd met in a barber shop. Orpath strung him along. George fell for it. However, there was something about George's style that appealed to Orpath, and at the proper moment so as not to embarass George, he took him into the fold.

George's whole life had been spent on the fringes of petty larceny. His father whom, surprise, surprise, he knew, was a member of the racetrack fraternity. He did tricks with horses at country fairs. Several of his charges died making the supreme effort. In Nebraska he was caught administering 'medicine' to a nag whose only chance lay in the proper use of the hypodermic.

George did not see his father again. The father died from an overdose of something himself in a Nebraska jail house. George's mother, seemingly relieved, ran off with a jockey, and George ended up in a 'home.'

Age sixteen, the recipient of a meager education, he started to fend for himself in the streets. He was a quick learner. By age twenty, he had become a streetwise con artist. This is what caught Orpath's eye in the barber shop.

Yes, one more big job, thought Orpath, and then

time to relax. His taut chin was evidence that the word 'relax' was a stranger to him. He placed a second call. This time to Minneapolis. "Harry," he told the phone's mouthpiece, "we are going one more time."

Without a pause he continued, "We'll use this place for headquarters. Make arrangements with the Reno National Bank." Arrangements would consist of a deposit to Orpath's account of something under a half million dollars and a letter of credit for whatever else might be needed.

Harry was Orpath's 'business man.' Whatever Orpath required was arranged without question.

He made a third call, this time to Philadelphia.

The number rang and was finally answered by a heavy voiced woman.

"Yeah."

"I'd like to speak with Mr. Wilton."

"Not here."

"Will you give me a number for him?"

"Who are you?"

"My name is Volta Orpath."

"Wait a minute while I check." Silence. Finally, "Yeah, your name is here. OK, try this." She gave him a Florida number.

He replaced the phone again and squinted the horizon. He would be three jumps ahead of George.

CHAPTER THREE

The next day in San Francisco, a 'shifty-looking' George Mortelli took a Harbor Tour. He took pictures, not of Alcatraz, not of harbor seals, not of other ships. He took pictures of the underpinnings of the Golden Gate Bridge. Some casual tourist from Kansas asked what he found so interesting about the underside of the bridge.

"Design," said George, and that was all. Slightly seasick, he returned to the dock. He went to the place where he had parked his car, and drove across the bridge again to his forest lair. After a week and a half of bridge photography, he had a complete set of detailed photographs showing every nut, bolt, and rivet. Now he had only to study the working habits of bridge employees. Painters, chippers, toll collectors, bridge police, drivers, garage mechanics. Bridge police particularly.

At one point, he walked across the bridge. On his way back, he stood a long time, watching the toll-collecting procedure. There was a small accident at one of the toll stations. Another, occasioned by a driver's effort to change lanes to avoid the hold-up at the damaged toll booth, affected two more lanes. Within a matter of minutes, cars were backed up out of sight.

Two big two trucks buzzed out of the bridge garage, and one of the damaged cars was removed without trouble. The others, however, were so jammed together that it took much longer. Traffic did not return to normal for nearly an hour. As he returned his camera to his case, George smiled. This type of traffic jam could be his friend.

To add to the toll problem, the Bridge Board had just raised the toll to $1.25. The poor toll-takers were busier than the proverbial one-armed paperhanger, making change.

This time, George went back to the hideaway, developed his film, and printed his enlargements. Then he headed for Sacramento and Reno. It was after six in the evening. He had packed his full collection of enlargements in the car trunk. He had also obtained a set of geodetic survey maps of everything within a 150-mile radius of the bridge. He was ready for the first planning session.

George decided to spend the night in Sacramento. He went to a motel on the outskirts of the city. While he slept, an explosion rocked one of the buildings used by the California State Controller's office. That explosion set off a trail of events which appeared to have no earthly connection with George Mortelli, his studio, or the Golden Bridge.

The explosion occurred during the early-morning hours, while the watchman was on his coffee break across the street. When asked what department had suffered in the accident, the watchman could identify it only as "Third Floor North."

Later in the morning, as George was leaving Sacramento, the newspapers were trying to get some pictures and an interview with State Controller Dory Eversharp. Eversharp wasn't exactly evasive about the work of the devastated office. But he wasn't very clear, either.

He described hundreds of persons who labored in

this section, and he had only praise for the work they did.

When asked who the head of the department was, he didn't know. Eversharp turned to his assistant, hoping to find the name of this paragon whom he had just extolled. The assistant didn't know.

Finally, the reporters went to the damaged area, and there found many displaced employees, wandering aimlessly.

There was very little left of the office space. One person interviewed told of his long career as a typist-file clerk. His work had mainly involved yellow copies, although at one point, he had become proficient with the filing systems used for second copies.

He did not know the subject matter of the materials which he filed.

Marian Ritter, another clerk interviewed, stated that the office did not deal with classified material. "My work was mostly developing budget reports to support the work of the section."

She added, "What I was told to put in the budget reports was difficult for me to understand, as it never seemed to reflect what the people in the office were doing."

"What were they doing?"

"Oh, I don't know that. All's I know is that they weren't doing what the budget was supposed to be paying for."

And so on, from one frustrating interview to another for the poor reporters. This frustration was compounded tenfold by the members of the Controller's staff who, try as they might, failed to find any explanation at all for the purpose of the bombed-out bureau.

The demise of this section was a sort of corpus delicti.

The newspapers did what they could with feature stories about desk remnants, twisted filing cabinets, mountains of unintelligible paper, and numerous boxes of cosmetic aids, such as secretaries keep in the bottom drawers of their desks.

"Sic transit gloria," thought Dory Eversharp, State Controller of California, but he did not say it.

Across the continent in sunny Florida, at a posh, but second-rate spa, the only explosion came in the form of the scantily-clad young woman who lay by the side of an azure and plastic swimming pool. She was soaking up the sun, while in turn she was being soaked up by an appreciative audience.

CHAPTER FOUR

Jeri loved the sun. She loved Florida. She loved herself. She particularly liked the way the sun sparkled off her well-oiled thighs.

One more dip and she'd dress for luncheon with her husband.

She was not letting her underlying concern over money intrude on this moment of warm comfort. Today was paid for — and tomorrow, too. What would happen to the balance of the week she didn't know, and for this moment, she wasn't going to think about it.

She rose, approached the diving board at the far side of the pool, and when she was sure that she had attracted the attention of at least two-thirds of the male population, she slipped into the water in what must be described as a perfect jack-knife dive.

She surfaced and swam easily to the end of the pool, where every man, in his heart of hearts, assisted her in leaving the water.

They were all ungrateful when she swathed herself in her voluminous terrycloth robe and left the area.

Jeri Wilton had been born Wilma Metz, in Utica, New York. In her day, the railroad train went down the main street like a trolley car.

Wilma was a bright and pretty girl. At age fourteen, she could change the saloon conversation in the time it took her to walk past the front door. Some girls just have it. Wilma had it. By the time she was sixteen, she was married to a drummer from one of the hat houses in New York City. Her parents had quickly consented. They knew an explosive situation when they saw one.

On one of her trips home, she met a good-looking architect, his hair neatly streaked with grey. Edwin Cooper Wilton. He sat next to her on the train. She never did get to Utica that time. Both of them left the train at Troy.

The drummer was quickly dumped. Wilma changed her name to Jeri. In fact, she changed it to Jeri Wilton. Legally. She also changed her style of living. Edwin was a good provider. As a young man he had been quite athletic. In the big city, he had to settle for the health-giving exercise offered by a bowling alley. He was very good at it, being so tall.

Jeri often joined Ed at the sport. She was a born competitor. As we have said, she was also bright. She wouldn't try to really compete with her husband at his sport. So, in her free time, she developed her own sport, at a shooting gallery. She was a natural. Soon she was competing. Then she became a champ.

She wasn't worried about Ed trying to compete at the pistol range. His eyes weren't right for that. They were just a little off-center.

Several of Wilton's potential clients did not question Wilton's capacity as an architect after Jeri mixed the drinks. In this regard she proved a great asset to him. Their life was a happy one until the man in Ed began to slow down.

Now she made her way through the pool entrance, and to an elevator which took her to the suite she and her husband could ill afford.

"Hi, Ed," she oozed, as she spotted Ed by the

phone. "You should have been there. The sun's great and the water is just right."

Ed didn't hear her. He was listening to the receiver and making notes on the phone pad.

She went into the shower.

Edwin Cooper Wilton was a big one. He'd been a minor football player at Stanford. He exuded confidence. People trusted him. They trusted him once too often.

He had been retained by the State of New Jersey to design and build a magnificent edifice to house the State Supreme Court. He worked on the plans for nearly two years. Finally, construction began. Halfway through, it became apparent to the contractor that some new financing was needed. This was unfortunate, because the need arose at the time the Arabs, through their oil-pricing policies, were having a noticeable effect on the interest rates. The contractor was desperate. He came to Wilton and told him that the building would never be completed unless certain changes were made in the specifications.

Wilton objected. He said that the suggested changes could be dangerous. The contractor pulled out a fat envelope and handed it to Wilton. Wilton didn't even look. He made the changes.

The day arrived when the world would see the wonders which had been wrought to better serve supreme justice. Unfortunately, too many people showed up, or at least, too many shared the main staircase at one time. It collapsed, and with it collapsed the professional career of Edwin Cooper Wilton.

He viewed the collapse from a balcony opposite. He made an instant decision. Hastily leaving the glistening monument through one of its lesser exits, he sped home, picked up his wife, his envelope, and their bags, and fled to the Bahamas.

He would be a 'wanted man.' This accident amounted to homicide. His photograph ended up in every police station and FBI office in the country. Finally, he made the Post Offices.

Eventually the excitement died down. Wilton's lawyers had developed an acceptable brief and plea which required Wilton's attendance at the penitentiary for a minimal term.

Wilton hung up the phone, but did not remove his hand from the receiver, as the sense of what he had heard coursed through his mind. He looked over at the bathroom door.

"Honey?" he invited. And out came Jeri as God and cosmetics had made her.

"Let's have lunch," she said.

"I have ordered it to be served on the balcony." Wilton smiled at his wife's unadorned beauty.

"Thoughty," complimented Jeri and she gave her husband a buzz on the top of his head. He responded by a casual pat on her well-rounded backside.

Just as she finished decorating herself into a loud and unrevealing muu-muu, the luncheon was brought by two refugee waiters. They soon had the sumptuous repast spread out on the balcony table. Ed quickly signed the check with an extra flourish.

"What's that for?" Jeri asked. Generally, Ed looked the bill over in every detail, carefully adding it himself and then writing in a ten percent tip. He was of the 'old' school. He was also a tight-wad.

At this point, he had no reason to be ungenerous, as he was about to reveal to Jeri over their first pina colada. He had thoughtfully put together a jug full of the creamy substance. He poured Jeri's glass and then his own, putting the jug back onto the side table

14

for future reference. When this ritual was completed, he took one long drink and looked out over the sea and said, "Jeri, we're going to be O.K."

"I hope so." Jeri took an introductory taste of the heaven-sent colada. She let Ed go on without asking the obvious.

"Some time ago, just after my 'vacation,' I met a young man who was very interested in my engineering background and somehow or other he had found out about my 'forced retirement.' I didn't pay much attention as the fellow looked like Brooklyn to me. He wanted me to meet his boss. I was on my way to meet you in Philadelphia. He gave me his boss's name and told me to expect a call. We exchanged phone numbers. Guess I didn't seem very enthusiastic because he mumbled something about 'some other time.' Well, the 'other time' was just a few minutes ago. When you came in, that phone call was from his boss."

"Yeah. What'd he want?"

"He — ah — has employment for me."

"Doing what, Eddie?"

Imagine that! Here these two were, down to their last credit card and she was being persnickety.

"I really don't know, but they want us to come out to Reno right now."

Jeri perked up at the name Reno.

"How's that going to happen? We don't even have taxi fare to get to the airport!"

There were times in Ed's association with Jeri that he felt like whacking her. This was one of them.

"Oh, come on Jeri. Don't rub it in. This is going to be all right. And, I may say, just in time."

"Sorry, Ed. My day for worrying was going to be tomorrow. Seriously, how do we do this?"

15

"We go to Reno. Money is being wired."

At the sound of the combination of Reno AND money, Jeri came alive.

"When?"

"Now."

After calls to make the plane reservations, bags were packed. The only flight they could get was early morning the next day.

Ed went down to the barber shop and was given 'the works.' Shiny-nailed, he went to the main Western Union office where his message was waiting.

The size of the amount had caused some consternation to the Western Union employee who had received Orpath's money order. However, he was able to put it together with the help of the Office Manager, who had access to the main safe.

The Wiltons retired early that night, and with a fair share of connubial enjoyment. Enough for Ed, if not for Jeri.

The next morning, with the sun, they were on their way West.

CHAPTER FIVE

As George drove on into Reno, he listened to the radio reports of a bombing in Sacramento.

He found his high-rise target and reported in at a fancy penthouse high above the desert.

After a wait, he was greeted by Orpath's friend and employee 'Puggo' Alexander. One look at Puggo's nose and you could understand 'Puggo.' One look at his cauliflowered ear and you'd understand what happened to his nose. He had been a B-26 pilot in World War II, before someone had knocked him cold in a Armed Forces Boxing Tournament. He wore a white coat, somewhat too large for him.

"Hi, George!" he squeaked in a surprising voice. "Let me give you a hand." He took up the big photo case George had leaned against the doorjamb.

"What the hell took you so long? Where's the boss?" George growled unpleasantly.

"Up front," squeaked Puggo, somewhat miffed at George's rudeness.

They headed in that direction. 'Up front' was an enormous living-room behind a bay of windows, framing the rooftops of Reno, the desert beyond, and the mountains beyond that.

The boss was engrossed in a TV game show, and did not turn to greet George, but gestured to a chair.

When the commercial came on, he turned the sound

off and looked at George. "It's about time," he observed.

"You will see that patience has paid off," George replied through a mouthful of chewing gum.

"I wish you wouldn't chew gum around me," the boss snapped petulantly. He stood up and walked to the bar, where he poured himself a glass of soda water.

"All right, let's see what you have," said the money and the brains.

George reached for the portfolio. Puggo beat him to it.

Together they opened it and put in on a little couch.

The first bridge picture was already on exhibit. It showed the great slab upon which the San Francisco tower rests.

Orpath grunted. He was rapidly calculating how much dynamite would be necessary to sink that pylon.

Next was a straight-up 'design' shot under the middle of the bridge. He surveyed the crisscrossing of girders. Several shots of the great cables and the smaller cables followed.

Some idiot was in the foreground of the next shot, smiling and out of focus. The cable terminal was clearly in focus and left no question as to its function.

So, on and on through thirty or more photographs. There were a few of the deck of the bridge, showing random automobiles crossing.

Orpath was not much impressed with the traffic-jam photographs.

"How do those idiots figure anyone will get out of San Francisco in an earthquake?" he asked himself.

"I'm hungry," George said.

"Food is in the pantry," Orpath invited, returning to his TV set.

He punched the sound button on as the game-show host cried out something about winning the $45,000 prize.

18

"We'll win far more than that," Volta Orpath said just under his breath.

George brought his sandwich back to the living-room and for a short while he watched the TV game show. Then he went to his room where he showered and changed his clothes.

"I'll go downstairs for a little while," he announced to Puggo, when he returned and saw that Orpath had retired for his before-dinner nap.

After George left, Puggo threw the deadbolt with an extra-heavy push.

The glitter of the casino, the clanking of the slot machines, the neat and tightly-covered derrieres of some of the guests all heightened George's sense of excitement. He moved through the crowd of inno-cents, crooks, police, callgirls, conventioneers, bank-ers, housepeople, losers and winners.

In all this crowd, he cut no swath. He melted into the noise and the light. His eyes narrowed. "Some-day," he thought.

He did like girls. Some liked him for a little while. Thought he was cute. Then, he'd get rough; use his heavy leather belt. After that, the girl was 'busy,' 'had a funeral to go to,' 'had to take care of a sick friend.' Finally, 'Scram, fellah, or I'll call the cops.'

These were not enduring friendships. But he'd have money. Plenty of it. Then the call would be dif-ferent. You just wait. Pigs. His eyes started to follow a blonde smoking a cigarette. She sauntered past him to be joined by a football player from Notre Dame or some place.

"The hell with it," sneered George. He went back to the penthouse and found Orpath dressed for dinner. They proceeded to dine at a table which had been set for the two of them, overlooking a carpet of two million lights. Some flashed, some were colored, some were just floating.

Puggo made drinks for them. Considering the outsized sleeves on his white coat, he did very well. A martini up for Orpath, and a bourbon and ginger for George. Neither one expressed gratitude.

Orpath opened the table conversation. "I just called our friend Ed Wilton and he will be here around noon tomorrow."

George had recommended his skills to Orpath during early discussions of the bridge plan. As Wilton was denied the right to work at his profession, and was nearly without funds, George thought he would be game for just about anything.

Dishonesty must, in time, flaw judgment, but it does not enervate skill. Wilton was skillful, and no one knew more about structural engineering than he.

Orpath congratulated George on his foresight relative to Ed Wilton. There was a lull in the conversation which did not invite interruption.

George looked across the table at Volta Orpath. "What little eyes," he thought. Then he noted his boss's tight, small mouth. Orpath's manner of eating was similar to those birds you see in the zoo, who look carefully with one eye at the anticipated bite, then make a quick movement and the food is gone. Not a particularly charming dinner companion.

But then, George himself had no corner on the charm market. You could say that they deserved each other.

They had greed in common. The game had worked for Orpath. He could have folded his tent and gone anywhere in the world to live out his life. Once into the greed business, though, one link forges the next. Reason has no appeal. A habit is a habit, and more begets more.

Hardly a word was spoken at dinner. Coffee was taken at the large boulder fireplace. Puggo was ordered to remove the dinner dishes, silver, and flatware. No word of appreciation The quality of the dinner was taken for granted. He disappeared. At least, it was a job.

Then Orpath looked over at George. "George," he said flatly, "this is a very tough project."

"It can be done," George repeated.

"Anything can be done," snorted Orpath.

"How much do you think we should ask for here?" George leaned forward.

"Not a cent less than $25 million," fell out of Orpath's tight mouth.

"Well, that will take care of a few drinks, certainly," George enthused.

Orpath went to the couch and began looking at George's photographs. He picked up one print at a time and held it under the light. Then he craned forward with his eye barely six inches away from the print's surface. You'd think he was looking for technical flaws in the photographs. He was counting rivets.

When he came to the toll plaza accident prints, he began looking into the pictured windows of stalled cars. Suddenly he said, "I don't believe it! Look at this! Here's some guy jumping a broad!" George came forward. Sure enough, in car six, there was a man and a woman completely oblivious to the scene, really gnawing at each other.

"You can't be too careful," George grinned, and looked again.

Orpath without any remark, went to the next photograph.

This was the one in which the person in the foreground was out of focus. The cable was still clear.

Orpath looked closely, and questioned, "How much weight do you think this holds?"

George peered. "I understand each of these cables can hold probably three, five or ten times more than is needed. I think the extra strength is unimportant, if the balance between the depending cables is substantially upset."

Orpath said quietly, "When we locate the vital pressure points, that fact must be demonstrated so clearly to our bankers that they won't quibble long about our capacity. I suppose that there are many crucial combinations of stress which could have that effect. Once we mention what we are doing there, I want these people to identify its importance as quickly as they would a pinched nerve."

"Wilton will do that for us," George said.

"Of course. Well, I wish we could do this with only Wilton." Orpath paused.

"We'll need an army," George remarked, as he looked closely at the photograph of the Marin tower.

Then he looked out at the two million lights. "Where will we find the people?"

"Tomorrow we'll get a handle on how many we may need from Wilton."

Orpath started to say something more, but paused, then said, "Terrorists?"

"Yeah, if we can find them," from George.

"Well, they've hijacked airliners. If the ante is high enough I don't see why they wouldn't help us do the same thing to the bridge."

George could see the beginning of an idea but he could also see a lot of trouble.

"Those guys are crazy."

"They must do some planning and thinking ahead."

"Who've you got in mind for starters?"

"Maybe some militant black group. Or some Arabs."

"Nah, the blacks would want too much and the Arabs are too far away. This isn't for them. No, we need someone who has a gripe right here. Something the Governor can grant when the heat's on him."

"You have a point," agreed Orpath.

"Who the hell is there?" George was hoping that by asking the question he would be shown the answer.

Orpath wondered about the Indians who took Alcatraz.

"You know, they just might do it," agreed George.

"No, on second thought I don't think so. Those Indians were motivated to grab land which they say had been theirs. It was sort of symbolic. There isn't anything symbolic about grabbing the bridge."

"Once we are on the bridge, I don't think we are going to need large numbers. We will need guys who know about dynamite. You know, where to put it and how to get it there."

"Yes," said Orpath. "I wasn't much impressed by what those people did once they were on Alcatraz. They made it a private fight and they took too long."

"We gotta be quick," George nodded. "In and out with the payoff."

"On the TV newscast, this fellow reported some building in Sacramento was blown up."

"I heard it on the radio this morning. Funny, I was there last night and I didn't hear any explosion."

"What time did they say it happened?"

"At three a.m."

"You were asleep."

"Yeah, guess that's why."

"Who did it?"

"No one seemed to know."

"Seems it all fits a pattern."

"Have there been others?"

"Yes, there have been. All in government buildings."

"Some sick taxpayer."

"Maybe. A lot of work for one man to do, though."

"Could be different cranks in different places."

"I don't think so and neither did the commentator. He seemed to think it is the work of some highly motivated group. The pattern as he discussed it suggested a well-organized attack on the government."

"Holy mackeral!"

"An odd thing happened the other day, and it's just beginning to make sense to me. You know, when you've been in the game as long as I have, you get to know a lot of different sorts of people. Safecrackers included."

"That wasn't any safecracker's job."

"Probably not. But, explosives were involved. Dynamite happens to be a safecraker's best friend."

"Of course."

"Well, Puggo told me he ran up against a fellow we have used several times in the past when we needed certain closely-guarded information. Top safecracker. Never touched. He told Puggo he was working for some sort of political organization which was into some pretty rough things."

"That fits. Did he give the name?" George queried.

"The fellow's no politician. Just does what he's told. Did say, though, that the group operated behind some kind of club front. STUB or STAG or something like that . . ."

"Well, that's a start."

"George, this man says he has traveled a lot with these people, and the towns he mentions have all ended up with a bombed-out government office."

"That's something."

"He said that the brains behind these excursions

is some tough guy whose name he did not know . . . that he never hesitates and seems to know exactly what he wants done."

George remembered the radio report he'd heard coming into Reno. "Say, I wonder if that fellow was in Sacramento last night."

"Could be the same bunch," volunteered Orpath.

"The report didn't say."

"Well, could be." Orpath was getting a little excited. He continued, "Maybe these are our people. You see, Puggo says some of them are in jail. If that's so, this might be the bait."

"Yeah, they'd want to get their buddies out of the slammer, all right."

"I wonder if these are the same people."

"We could try to find out, Volta."

"Yes, I think we should. If it's true, we can use them, and they can use us." Orpath's eyes reflected the firelight.

"Volta, you beat all! Of course, this is the answer! I was thinking about the American Indians, like you said, on Alcatraz. But this idea is better. And, I think these guys can work better. Besides, since their buddies are in jail, this way they get their pals out!" George patted a pleased Orpath on the back.

The lights were dimming and the moon made the mountain a great black ascending line on the horizon.

"I am tired now," said Orpath.

"And well he should be," thought George. He equated mental activity with fatigue.

Next morning Reno was muggy and yellow-gray.

George was so excited by Orpath's clear idea that the weather didn't bother him. He went off to the Reno Library to find out what he could about activist organizations.

CHAPTER SIX

George found the Reno Library a very confusing place. A young librarian, recognizing a lost soul, came to his assistance and before he knew it she had shepherded him into the nether world of criminal activism, at least as far as the library filing system provided. Then she had led him into the stacks where he had to make a stern choice: the girl or the information. The animal in George crept very close to the surface. The spell, however, was broken by the intrusion of the chief research librarian who asked Miss Helpful some housekeeping question, the answer to which dispelled the fantasy.

The young librarian straightened herself up, gave a push to her hair and proceeded to put young Mister Georgie on the trail of STAB, which was the closest thing to the safecracker's STUB or STAG.

Within two hours, George had not only a long list of current articles covering STAB leaders, but he also had xeroxes of at least thirty news reports of meetings, demonstrations, petitions, and work stoppages. He was surprised that there was so much written about STAB that he had never seen before.

With an airy wave of the hand to his pretty and frustrated assistant, George went whistling out of the library, arriving at the penthouse in time to leave for the airport to meet Edwin Cooper Wilton.

When he and Puggo arrived at the airport, George hopped out and curtly ordered Puggo to wait.

Bustling, noisy, crowded with the color of ten thousand Hawaiian-shirt designs, the airport did not greet George as if it knew him. It didn't.

He pushed his way to the gate which Wilton would use. He waited.

George remembered that Ed Wilton was tall. As he waited, he let his eyes stray in the direction of several ambling young women. No one noticed, not even the girls.

"You wait," thought George.

Then the big 747 rolled its cumbersome bulk to the ramp and stopped, just as it seemed about to come right into the waiting room.

After a dozen people cleared the ramp exit, a very tall, well-dressed, grey-haired man came toward him.

"Hi, Wilton, how are you?" George advanced pleasantly.

"Marvelous, just marvelous," returned Wilton. George noticed that Wilton was followed by an attractive woman wearing heavy mascara.

George looked at her face, which was a change in his approach pattern. He had to look at her face because her full lips were speaking to him.

"Oh, George," she gushed. "I've heard all about you!"

George smiled. "I hope not *all* about me."

"Well, enough," she said.

Wilton was a little taken aback by this interchange.

"George," he introduced, "this is my wife, Jeri."

"Hi, Jeri." George put out his hand and made an instant friend.

Wilton was looking around at the array of shirts, children, hats, people, carry-on luggage. He wore a peculiar expression, as if he'd rather be somewhere else. George was to find that that was Wilton's usual look.

All of them started to move with the crowd to the baggage area.

Everything reclaimed, they went to the car which Puggo had kept at the curb.

George helped Mrs. Wilton into the car, while Wilton folded himself beside her. George climbed into the front seat, staring at Mrs. Wilton's knee and upper thigh. Her dress had caught on the velour seat and, being an informal person, she had made no effort to re-cover her exposed nether extremity.

Wilton missed all this byplay while trying to lower the window.

"Very hot here," he observed as Puggo jerked away from the curb.

"Muggy," George corrected.

The drive took twelve minutes.

The conversation, which had been so brisk, did not pick up again in the confines of the limousine. Puggo's cauliflower ear had caught Jeri's eye. Puggo noticed her interest through the rearview mirror. He didn't smile.

At last they rolled into the garage.

Puggo said he would see to the luggage.

George took Mrs. Wilton's elbow and guided her to the elevator.

"Does this place have a casino?" she asked.

"A big one," George said, squeezing her arm a little harder.

"I'd like to see it," she gushed.

"You'll see it all right," Wilton snapped, "but with your own dough!"

"Yeah," said Jeri.

After some delay, they trooped into the elevator for a ride to the 39th floor.

Puggo greeted them at the door, white coat and all. He was not breathless. "The service elevator must be very fast," George thought.

Jeri took the place in with one long look, seemed satisfied, and put down her all-purpose bag. Wilton put his hat on the reception table and asked where Orpath was.

"Mr. Orpath will be with you in a moment," Puggo announced.

They all walked to the view. George pointed out some landmarks. Then Orpath came in.

Introductions and small talk. Orpath was not a ladies' man, but he was pleasant enough on this occasion.

The contrast between the size of Wilton and that of Orpath was not lost on George. He did not find any contrast at all between himself and Wilton. But contrast there was. Wilton was the size of both of them put together.

Orpath eyed his tall partner, then eyed his wife. George thought he noticed a slight shake of the head.

Dinner would be served at seven. Until then, everyone was free to do whatever.

George's fantasy was not far behind Jeri's. However, with much talk of taking naps and catching up on time-lag, Wilton and his wife went up to their room.

"He's a big one," said Orpath.

"Let's hope he has a brain to match his size."

"Let's hope."

CHAPTER SEVEN

Although the Society to Abolish Bureaucracy had not been officially connected with the caper at the State Controller's building, the FBI in Sacramento had concluded that it could have been involved. Enough had been said about the organization by this time that it was referred to by its acronym, STAB.

The trouble was that nothing had incriminated STAB. Its members talked loudly against the bureaucracy and held mass meetings. They published pamphlets. They even bought TV time. But STAB's stated policy was against inciting anything illegal.

The group's policy statement did speak out against a strangling bureaucracy's threat to American freedom. They supported candidates for public office. All this, STAB's parent organization, the League for Better Government, had done over a period of at least a decade.

STAB had been established as the militant wing of the more staid League for Better Government. It picketed, and organized strikes and slowdowns. Its leaders held massive public meetings. When newspapers bleated for the bureaucracy, effective boycotts were undertaken.

STAB's leader was an inspired man named Lauris Vandingan. Probably once was Van Dingan. He was a stocky man who, in his youth, could have been a wrestler. His blond hair and his sky-blue eyes gave a first impression of softness. The slight smile which seemed to be perpetually on his lips suggested friendliness.

It was when you considered his chin and heard him speak that you realized this was a man of enormous strength.

His voice never faltered. Its tone demanded immediate attention. The chin guaranteed complete dedication to what was said. No one had been able to lay a glove on him personally.

Certain of his confederates, however, had not been so lucky. Eleven of them were in jail in California on various charges having little or nothing to do with STAB's political pursuits.

Although some of its leaders had been picked up, everything STAB did as an organization seemed to be within the law.

Agent Benjamin Franklin Friendly of the FBI district office in Sacramento was not so sure.

STAB chief Lauris Vandingan had graduated from Harvard University, summa cum laude. His field was government. His Ph.D. had been won with a thesis which dug deep into the oligarchy known as the Veterans Administration.

Former President Hoover, who had been asked by President Truman to head a group studying the problem of government agencies, was so impressed with Vandingan's paper that he secured a staff appointment for the young Ph.D.

Although Vandingan did not often see or speak with the former President, he was conscious of the man's insight and foresight. He was also conscious that Mr. Hoover and his Commission were fighting an uphill battle to simplify the government.

31

The seed of everything Lauris Vandingan was to become was nurtured in this garden of hope.

As one of the better-educated staff members, much of the preliminary investigation was assigned to him. Normally, he found the government employees he interviewed open and even voluble about the demands of their tasks.

To a person, however, they all wanted extra help.

When pushed by Vandingan to support their requirements, many became evasive. Some were completely dishonest in providing support statistics.

Vandingan came away from his association with Mr. Hoover's Commission a troubled man.

The Korean War gave him more reason to be troubled.

He was drafted, and through the most incomprehensible bungling of records, he ended up as a dental assistant. He requested front-line duty, and was assigned to a headquarters communications center as a driver.

Finally, with the Korean stalemate, he was sent home. He went to work for a small college in Ohio, where he taught government. Many of his students were on the GI Bill. The brighter ones peppered Vandingan with questions. The excess. The tax structure. The duplication. The red tape.

Having recently tried doing business with the Veterans Administration, these students had some first-hand experience to draw upon.

And so, Professor Vandingan, already a man sensitive to those problems, found himself propelled toward activism. He sat on committees. He chaired committees. He sought funding for special studies. He found a generous and friendly reception among the right-wing industrial-complex types. These men were, of course, supporting a reduction of bureaucratic red tape, to better carry out their various pursuits without government supervision or intervention.

Vandingan, excited by the fact that he had allies against the burgeoning complexities of government, did not immediately recognize the uncharitable interests of his supporters.

When he did, he was being borne along by a tide too swift to resist.

He adopted the philosophy, not unlike George Washington in his early revolutionary days, that the end justified the means. He accepted violence as a tool. Violence against the palaces of bureaucratic privilege. The enclosures, the computers, the desk chairs, the filing systems: these were the soldiers of the enemy.

Orpath stumbled across Vandingan's path at the moment when STAB was trying to make the government, both federal and state, face up to the charges. STAB was the true defender of American liberty. This fight was against the idea of extended government. By some subcutaneous sense, the government was slowly coming to understand the seriousness of STAB's attacks.

With no serious and straightforward effort of its own to protect itself at either federal or state level, the government was trying to accomplish by indirection that which it could not attack directly and constitutionally.

The State of California had, for example, imprisoned eleven active STAB leaders on the flimsiest of excuses, ranging from tax evasion to drunken driving.

CHAPTER EIGHT

Benjamin Franklin Friendly in Sacramento punctured his wall map with a red tack, marking the position of the State Controller's Building.

Friendly was the local FBI bomb expert. He gave the tack an extra push. He was frustrated.

This explosion fit the pattern of the previous ones.

He thought that the FBI should be mounting an investigation, right now. For some reason, the California Governor had not seen fit to invite the FBI into the picture. There was some legal hang-up as to whether the FBI could go ahead without his authority.

Although there had been explosions involving bureaucratic redoubts across the country, nothing seemed directly connected to the events in California.

Friendly's Chief had counseled patience, asking Friendly to monitor developments closely, so that when the FBI was invited in, a minimum of time would be wasted in the start-up.

Friendly was an agent of the old school. He was not the 'new breed.' He plodded. He was a bulky man. Once, he had been slim and eager. Proximity to retirement found him ready for it.

He was respected, but he had never advanced to the top job.

His wife was a nice, quiet little lady. She had been an Army nurse. They'd met overseas while he was on military-police duty, and she was assigned to a station hospital.

His FBI experiences before the War won him his Captain's bars. He had been commended several times but he was not promoted.

So now, he was pushing thumb tacks.

No sooner had Agent Friendly given the thumb tack the extra push than his phone rang.

"Friendly, will you please come up?" It was the voice of the District Director.

"Yes, Sir," said Friendly.

In the Chief's office, two other men, from the Governor's staff, were sitting. They were asking about the most recent bombing, and requesting FBI information.

"I'd like to take a closer look at STAB," Friendly responded when asked what he thought should be done.

"They're a bunch of loudmouths," said one of the Governor's men.

"They certainly appear to have made noise," Friendly agreed.

"Do you think they'd have the nerve to make these attacks on our property?" asked the second man.

"Everything they say is certainly aimed against the government." Friendly tried not to be negative. "I suppose no one should be surprised at whatever else they might aim at the government."

The District Director said, "Friendly, I think we should take on some preliminary duty here. Not go too far, mind you, but at least get our feet wet."

It was the opening that Friendly had hoped for.

"Yes, Sir," agreed Friendly. "You are absolutely right, but not go *too* far, just get our feet wet."

It was a beginning.

CHAPTER NINE

As the sun went down, lights had been put on in the spacious penthouse living-room by the white-coated Puggo. The conspirators-to-be would gather before the great fireplace at seven.

Ed Wilton had been the first to arrive, and he'd made himself a drink. Then Orpath came in.

"Ed," he inquired, "are you folks comfortable?"

"Heavens, yes," beamed Wilton.

"Need anything, just tell Puggo and he'll arrange it."

There was a moment of silence between them, then Orpath said, "Ed, if this thing goes, we'll be on our way to a real fortune."

"I hope I can be helpful."

"You will be. You are a very important part of the trip."

Wilton swelled a little. He knew that he was the technical brains, but he didn't mind hearing it said.

"I'm going to try to do my part," he smiled at the small man.

"You will, I'm sure."

"How much will there be when we're done?" Wilton ventured.

"We haven't decided exactly yet, because we may have a weight problem."

"What do you mean by that?" Wilton asked.

"I think we should be paid in gold." Orpath sat down.

"Well?" from Wilton.

"There's a transportation problem," he answered. He steepled his fingers.

"I see."

"I think we know how to do it, but we haven't settled the detail logistics," Orpath explained.

Just then Jeri came in, looking like a spring bouquet.

"My, my, you fellows look handsome against the sunset! Make mine a gin over, Jocko," she tossed to the sad-faced Puggo, who had just come to the bar. He winced.

"Good evening, Mrs. Wilton," Orpath rose and greeted her politely, baring his protruding teeth with a small smile.

"Call me Jeri," she smiled.

"OK, Jeri." Orpath became friendly.

He turned to Wilton and asked, "No offense, Ed, but what is Jeri supposed to do in this business?"

"Well, in the first place, I seldom go anywhere without her, and in the second, she's very fast with a gun. She's sort of my bodyguard."

"Yeah," said Jeri. "I'm women's pistol champ in New Jersey, and I knocked off some ribbons in Chicago, Cleveland, and Albany, as well."

Wilton looked very pleased at his wife's recitation.

"Well, you could have fooled me," said Orpath.

"Not after I've fired a round or two." Her eyes surveyed the room for an imaginary target.

"Tomorrow, tomorrow," Orpath cried hastily, "at a shooting gallery."

Jeri laughed. "What's the matter, thought I'd pull an Annie Oakley, didn't you? Everything in its place, Charlie." Orpath nodded. He thought he had saved the day, or at least one of the picture windows.

"You know, if you do the job right at the rifle range, you can win a bundle if the betting jerks are around," she added, with a wink.

Orpath's small mouth fought to smile. Wilton had that 'wish-I-were-someplace-else' look on his face.

Jeri downed her drink. Puggo had the glass away from her hand and at the bar before Jeri could get out, "All right, if you insist."

Just as Jeri finished her remarks George sauntered up to the group in a neat black suit, frilled shirt, and a large, dark-blue bow tie. He was paying the lady a compliment. He'd dressed. He'd picked up what she said about the rifle range.

"Honey, I'll take you down to the range and I'll have just the right suckers lined up. Don't shoot too good to start, and we'll lose a little here and there. Then, we'll knock 'em."

"George, you funny little guy, that's exactly what we'll do!" And she patted him on the head.

"Puggo, a bourbon and seven."

It was a jolly group. Dinner passed, with Jeri eating a great deal. George eyed her portions, figuring that a sharpshooter probably had to eat to have energy.

After dinner, Orpath revealed the set of photographic enlargements. Ed Wilton stepped forward like a judge at a photographic exhibition. He looked at everything two or three times.

"If we are going to hit, we must work on those two pylons and the suspension balance."

He looked at the geodetic survey.

"You know," he ruminated, "when this bridge was first thought about, there was great contention between the bridge's engineer, Joseph B. Strauss and a professor down at Stanford, a well-known geologist, who said this structure would never hold in a 1906-type earthquake."

Orpath looked at him. "If it won't hold in a heavy earthquake, it for damn sure wouldn't hold out against some well-placed dynamite."

"Who was the guy at Stanford?" asked Jeri with some interest.

"His name was Willis, Bailey Willis. He put his whole reputation on the line."

"What happened to him?"

"He died, not satisfied, and, I'm sure, unhappy that his theory had never really been put to the test. When I was at Stanford, he had retired and was given the job of taking care of the gardens in the Stanford Quad."

Orpath suggested, "If this Willis felt as deeply as you say, he might have written something on the subject."

Jeri was right with him. "Yeah," she said, "he probably put his finger right where the damn thing would fall apart."

Wilton looked at his wife with appreciation.

"Gee, babe, you're cute when you're serious."

"Listen to me, Ed. If this bozo was a professor, he wrote and he spoke. We just have to uncover his stuff on the bridge."

Orpath smiled. His little mouth really strained. This gal was a find. He then asked George to re-check the library for material on Bailey Willis. George made a note of the name.

After a few minutes of silence, Jeri put her glass down. "Where's the casino?" she asked, like a child who thought she'd be denied.

"Right here in the building," George volunteered.

"I'm going to bed," announced the graying Wilton.

"I'm going to stake you," said Orpath to Jeri, and he gave her a roll of bills.

"I'm going to take you," smiled George, and he did.

39

As the others dispersed, he and Jeri climbed into the waiting empty elevator and started the trip to the casino level. Jeri seemed relieved to be free of the penthouse. She sort of leaned against George; just enough to get the fire started.

The elevator stopped at the twenty-first floor, and the door opened. No one. Before the door could close, George had invited Jeri to get off with him at this stop to view the desert from the twenty-first. There wasn't much difference between the view on the twenty-first and what they'd seen from the penthouse, except that as they stood at the twenty-first-floor window, they were alone.

Jeri did not waste time taking in anything but George.

He started to look out the window on a conditioned reflex, and met full force the face, lips, and warm breath of Jeri.

That is not all he met.

For what seemed a short eternity, they stood as one in the faded sunset. Each delighted in the other's animal traits. The casino was as forgotten here as in some hilltop monastery. Who needs to gamble when the prize is yours before the game begins?

The conversation did not make much sense. It did, however, reflect the surprise, joy, anticipation and excitement of discovery. These two were not novices. They were case-hardened. They knew who they were and what they were doing, and there wasn't much doubt about what they were going to do to each other.

There are moments like this which, for absolutely every reason, should never take place.

Separating what had passed between them from life already lived and the rest yet to come would be like ungluing the sun.

They regarded each other with mutual gratitude

and slowly moved apart, the distance of the heat between them.

George was the first to speak.

"Jeri," he whispered.

"George," she breathed in refrain.

They agreed to head for the casino, but the enthusiasm for that game was spent.

Little George had become Big George, and Jeri was only beginning.

On the way back to the penthouse, in their own elevator away from the world, they embraced and smiled.

"Patience," said Jeri.

"Patience," said George.

That either of these people would know the word 'patience' is surprising. More surprising is the fact that in their present state of mind they would think of it at all. The rug in front of the boulder fireplace appealed to Jeri. His own bedroom appealed to George.

As the elevator door opened, darkness greeted them. The lighting had been turned low in the penthouse's front room.

"George," Jeri said distinctly and, he thought, loudly, "what a pleasant evening, even if I didn't manage to win anything!"

"Uh-huh," said George.

"Goodnight, Georgie, see you tomorrow." And Jeri disappeared into the shadows which led to the Wiltons' room.

George just stood there.

CHAPTER TEN

As George, in his early-morning dream, struggled with what he thought was Jeri, Friendly was shaving in Sacramento. He aimed to get to his office very early, so that he could have a conversation with one of his old friends in the Department in Washington.

His friend was an expert on terrorist groups. It was possible he might help to put together the make.

Friendly arrived at his office at 6:25, just in time to catch his friend at 9:30 Washington time.

"Jack, Ben Friendly."

"Hiya Ben. What's up?"

"I really don't know, but I thought I should check in with the master."

"Anytime."

Ben Friendly then told him all he knew about the Controller's Building explosion and the California Governor's recent request for information. He also touched on some of the other explosions. He related his suspicions about STAB.

"Well," said Washington, "sounds to me like you have a live one."

"You really think so?"

"Yep."

"Why?"

"Well, these fellows in STAB seem to have done

42

a hell of a lot of yelling, and," he added, "they've really been ignored."

"That's right," said Friendly.

Washington said, "Now, you yell a lot and no one pays any attention, then you finally kick someone in the shin."

"Makes sense."

"That's what happened."

"What's the next step?"

"Start following these guys."

"We could do that. Pick them up at their meetings and just stay with 'em. Eventually one of them will bring some firecrackers."

"Firecrackers?"

"Well, you know, dynamite."

Friendly put the phone back and looked out his window. "Firecrackers!" he said out loud.

He could set up the team. But he must be careful. He must not go 'too far.' It occurred to him that dynamite was going pretty far.

That night, someone played with firecrackers at Sitting Wells, Nevada. A whole administration building at the testing site disappeared from the face of the earth.

At first, it was thought that something had gone wrong with the explosives stored at the site. Actually something had gone wrong with them, but that was only because something else happened first.

News reports and TV coverage called it an accident. Government P.R. men were very persuasive.

CHAPTER ELEVEN

Orpath, anxious to get things started, asked the Wiltons and George to sit with him after breakfast. He wanted to go into some preliminary detail.

When they arrived in his study off the main living-room; he was looking at the survey maps. The photographs were on a settee near-by.

"Well, well, well," he began, as he cleaned his glasses. "So much to do, and so little time to get it done."

"No time like the present," George said.

"Right, right," agreed Orpath.

Wilton then added the understatment of the day, and it was early yet. As he sat down, he said, "This job is going to take more than a blowtorch."

"It's going to take a lot of things," responded Orpath. "Let's go through what we want to do, then we'll start a list of what we'll need."

George began to enumerate. "In the first place, our aim is to collect $25,000,000. We gotta scare the California dudes into providing these goodies."

"Yeah," said Jeri. "And then we have to get away."

What a down-to-earth type!

"Yes, we do; we have to get away," George nodded.

"$25,000,000 and a getaway. It's as simple as that," Orpath summed up.

Wilton, pretending to ignore the magnitude of the

amount, ventured, "We must inform them that we've wired certain key points of the bridge with dynamite, which can be electronically detonated."

George asked, "Won't they send people to defuse?"

Wilton said, "I am sure they will, but we tell them this'll only set the whole thing off sooner."

"Then we instruct them about the gold payment," added Orpath, whose aquisitve mind was never far from the payoff.

Wilton continued, "I think delivery could be made at the San Francisco Airport and loaded onto a large and fast plane. When we get there, we take off."

Orpath just looked at him. "Yes," he said, "along with every Air Force plane in the western U.S."

Wilton was not to be dissuaded. "I said we'd have a *fast* plane."

Orpath agreed that a fast plane would be needed. The question was how to get from the bridge to the plane.

Some consideration was given to the use of police cars and hostages. This would require the carrying of a remote control detonator. The threat of the detonator would discourage close pursuit.

No one could meddle with the explosive instrumentation until the remote control devise was deactivated by Wilton. That would not happen until everyone was clear and the gold was in hand.

Orpath was not sold on the idea. Neither was George.

Then throaty-voiced Jeri threw in, "Why not have the helicopter right on the bridge itself? Once loaded, we head for the airport carrying the remote control with us."

Orpath shook his head. "The complete break has to be made at the bridge." His voice was firm.

George looked at him. "How do we get away?"

"By plane, right from the deck of the bridge!"

"How the hell do you avoid the traffic?" Wilton asked.

"Won't be any traffic," said Orpath.

"Just how do you arrange that?" asked George.

Wilton became sarcastic. "Oh, easy. You just tell the Bridge Authority that we have a ton of dynamite right in the middle of the bridge. They'll stop the traffic fast enough."

Orpath ignored him. "The traffic will be stopped, all right. We'll fix it so that no one, from any direction, will try to come onto the bridge. We'll barricade it."

"Yeah!" from George.

Wilton said, "What will the authorities be doing while we are building the barricades?"

Orpath explained, "It will happen so fast that they won't know about it until after it's happened."

"Ah," said Wilton, "shock troops?"

"More or less."

Orpath then told George to pull the photographs showing the bridge deck.

George found the enlargements showing the bridge roadway leading to San Francisco from Marin. Then he found a corresponding one, leading in from Doyle Drive, San Francisco. Between the two of these photographs, one could see four-fifths of the bridge floor.

Orpath began to describe his idea of the barrier. Simultaneously, armed vehicles would come from both directions to form the barriers These would block all lanes at each end of the bridge, at the San Francisco tower, and at the same time, the Marin side. If, by chance, there was any traffic on the bridge, it would be cleared, one way or another, before the barricade was completely in place.

"Day or night?" queried George.

"Daytime would create terrible problems," Orpath cautioned. "A foggy, rainy, windy night will do the trick."

"Rain. That will be nice for the dynamite," sneered Wilton, slumping into a chair.

"Now, look, Ed — Volta has put this thing on wheels. You just find the spots, and we'll worry about the explosion."

Wilton scowled over at George. "All very well for you to pass off this concern about wet fuses, but if the damn thing misfires, you'll blame me."

"Won't be the first time you've been blamed," from Jeri.

A terrible look crossed Wilton's face.

Orpath stepped in.

"Now, now," he said, "we're trying to find answers."

George, recalling his experience on the bridge during the toll plaza accident, explained that in all probability within two minutes, bridge personnel would know that something was wrong; and within three to four minutes, a police vehicle would be on its way to clear the problem.

Orpath felt it an inconvenience that would pose only an expected problem which heavy guns would take care of. It would be the last mission of car and officers. Similar precautions would be taken at the Marin end of the bridge although it was possible that there would be no police in the vicinity.

Orpath suggested that loudspeakers would be needed to order oncoming vehicles to turn back. As no one would be using the oncoming-vehicle lanes, there would be plenty of space to negotiate the U-turns.

Then George suggested the problem which presented itself if some irate citizen started to push through; the same fate as the police car.

During this period, George described how the radio section would be in contact with the highway patrol, and the demands would be made.

Wilton sat back with grudging admiration.

His wife said, "Jeest!"

Orpath had closed his eyes. "Then?" he questioned.

"Then," George continued, "we start our work, tying off various areas which you, Ed, will identify. Our targets actually should be quite simple," he explained. "The hardest job, according to Ed, will be going through the floor of the bridge at two key places."

"That's right," said Wilton.

"We repeat our demands; with great detail, we tell them what we propose to do." George became explicit. "We warn them not to try approaching the bridge from any direction. Ed, can we use electronic signals to activate light explosives?"

"Yes, yes, of course we can," Wilton agreed.

"Here is where we need the extra help," sighed Orpath.

"The 'army.' Without it, the job will be impossible. It will probably involve twenty or thirty other people," Wilton figured.

"If you involve other people, even three, how are you going to keep your plans secret?" Jeri asked from her big plush chair by the window.

"We think we've found the group," George explained.

"Who?" asked Wilton.

"They call themselves 'Society to Abolish Bureaucracy, STAB,'" George began.

"Oh, I've heard of them," Jeri joined in. "STAB. They were on TV."

48

"A lot of their leaders are in jail, and some are charged with very serious offenses," George continued.

Orpath began, with a little laugh, "Yes," he said. "Among other things, I think they're the ones who've blown up several public offices. They did such a good job that not even the number on the office door was left. The newspapers had a hell of a time in Sacramento a couple of days ago, identifying just which office had been blown up. It seems that no two employees worked on the same subject matter. All they knew was that it was in the State Controller's building."

Orpath added, "Seriously, if these jobs were done by STAB, we'd be lucky if they'd join us. They must have superb leadership to get away with these things!"

"We'll just have to make contact with them," said Jeri, the great socializer.

George produced his news clippings, and there was general agreement that this group would be just right, whether or not its members were responsible for the bombings.

The discussion had covered the complete morning and the idea was taking shape.

They adjourned for lunch.

At the newsstand downstairs, George bought a newspaper to check the racing results of the day before. A big article on the front page announced the demise of the Sitting Wells test center.

"Wowie," he exclaimed. "Our 'army' is getting close to home."

Orpath read the news report carefully, nodded his head, and cracked a small smile.

"I like these people," he remarked.

CHAPTER TWELVE

Benjamin Franklin Friendly now did what George had already done. He went to the library, and came away with practically the same material George had in his possession.

When he returned to his office, he piled the material on the table in front of him.

He then began a list of meeting dates, arrests, demonstrations, headquarters, addresses, names, ages, and general references.

That done, he started working on his file of explosion incidents, both in California and elsewhere.

Every time the leader, Vandingan, surfaced, this was put into the mix.

By the middle of the afternoon he had put together a comprehensive history on two subjects: the Society to Abolish Bureaucracy, and recent explosion incidents.

Bleary-eyed, he was still excited by what he was doing.

When the phone rang, it was his Chief.

"Well, Ben, have you started yet?" came through the earpiece.

"Yes, Sir."

"Careful. Don't go too far."

"No problem."

It wasn't any problem, yet. It was all in Benjamin

Franklin Friendly's head, and his little office. That was not going too far.

Friendly hung up his phone. No sooner had the connection been broken than an office boy tossed the evening paper in front of him.

"If it's explosions you want, how do you like this?" and he banged the door as he left.

Friendly glanced down at the printed page. It looked like eight others that he had just finished trying to analyze. Trying to catch some twist. Trying to see a shadow. If he saw a shadow, he knew light would be close behind.

The light was in Nevada.

Sitting Wells, Nevada. He'd never heard of it. Those traveling nearby at 2:30 a.m. certainly heard of it. Anyone within five miles heard of it; those closer to the site were lucky not to be cut up by flying shards of former windowpanes.

Friendly read on. No one seemed sure about the purpose of this test site. The newspapers, all wishing to keep their proper place, did not unleash their inquiring reporters, for fear of uncovering some terrible state secret.

It was enough for Benjamin Franklin Friendly. It was also Friday afternoon. He called his wife.

"Honey, pack a quick bag for each of us. We're going to Reno!"

"Reno?" came over the phone.

"Yes, Reno.

"Oh, Ben, you remembered!"

"Remembered? Oh, yeah. Well, you get the bags packed. I'll be there in half an hour. I want to look at some distressed real estate."

Just as Ben was leaving, his phone rang. He just kept going.

His wife had packed up and was ready to go.

"Ben," she said, "you are an old spoofer."

He started the car and drove down the street.

Just then, the sun broke through, and he remembered.

"Honey," he smiled, "it's been a long time, and what a wonderful time, and you made it that way, and today is *the* day."

"You were so funny. Do you remember? You had to go off on some kind of emergency and you yelled over your shoulder as you left, 'Honey, we'll get married when I get back!' Ben, you hadn't even asked me!"

"Well, you said 'yes' fast enough."

"Ben, dear, it's been so good."

"Thanks, Honey."

They were on the highway heading east into the mountains.

Ben brought her up to date on the latest events. He told her that his office was dragging its feet. He knew that some fast action would be needed, even if he had to do it on his free time.

So, off to Reno they went, she to celebrate her 25th anniversary, he to track down some terrorists, *and* to celebrate their 25th.

Next morning, early, Ben went out to the Sitting Wells test site. What he saw convinced him that there wouldn't be any testing there for some time to come.

He listened to some 'refugees,' but what they said didn't make sense. No one seemed to have any idea as to what the function of the site had been, except that explosives were stored there. No one had seen anyone. Not surprising, as whoever attacked the place did it when all the workers were home, or supposed to be, and behind the backs of the guards, if any.

The guard, it turned out, had suffered an injury. He had cut his hand three miles away, trying to leave a house belonging to the manager of the local Chamber of Commerce. The manager was out of town, and his wife was lonely. The guard was just trying to do his civic duty.

Later, Friendly would try to piece together what had happened at the test site.

Finally, he went back to the hotel and found his wife very pleased with herself. She had hit a silver-dollar jackpot. The trip was paid for.

They walked around, looking at the lights.

They approached a large shooting gallery.

"Come in here, Honey, and I'll show you that your Uncle Dud hasn't lost his touch."

They looked through the big, windows and then they entered.

He located the area set aside for .45 caliber shooting. Honey winced at the noise. He was proving himself.

Just then, George, Wilton, and Jeri took the range just down from Friendly.

Friendly noticed this. Rather, he noticed Jeri. No man on his 25th should be shown a girl who looks like Jeri looked.

Ben missed a few targets.

Jeri gave an exhibition of what she could do.

Out of the corner of his eye, he saw some padded-pinstripe type step up and offer to shoot against her.

Would she mind?

"Of course not," smiled Jeri.

Ben noticed that his wife had turned to watch. "This is going to be good," he said.

The pinstripe was a local favorite. Quite a crowd gathered. Some dark-haired little guy was taking the bets.

The girl shot sporadically. Won some, lost a lot.

The pikers were pushed to the rear, and the real

sugar stepped forward to make betting history. The bets were astronomical. And, she was losing.

Ben was just ready to leave, when zap-zap-zap, the pinstripe was biting the dust.

Ben stopped in his tracks. The babe was raking up a fortune.

Benjamin Franklin Friendly looked over at what had been a massacre, and he looked straight into the face of Ed Wilton.

Friendly nearly said hello. He recognized the man.

There was a lot of pushing and shoving, and in the excitement, they were separated.

On their way back to the hotel, Friendly told his wife, "I saw a fellow there I'm sure I know, but I can't place his name. I know he's a construction man, and that's as far as I can go."

"Don't worry, dear. They seemed to win a lot of money, and that should make them all very happy."

"Yes," sighed Friendly.

Puggo drove George, Wilton, and Jeri 'home.'

George had collected a cool $78,586, and, as Mrs. Friendly had predicted, they were all very happy.

Joking, George deducted the money for his 'fee' and gave the balance to Jeri, who gave it to Ed Wilton, who looked, for once, as if he were glad to be where he was.

That evening before dinner, George noticed that Jeri was as flushed with victory as if she had taken an amphetamine. She was all over the place. Orpath watched her with some surprise. He had no idea that a shooting gallery could do this to a person.

Puggo made drinks for everyone and served some little hors d'oeuvres which were one of his specialities.

Then dinner.

Orpath wanted to get down to business right away. He had spent the afternoon with George's clippings about STAB. He raced through his meal, excused himself, and went into his study.

The others hastily finished what they had left and joined him.

When they gathered around him, he tapped the collection of xeroxes. "Our answer is here," he exclaimed.

George thought he was being hasty. "Don't you think we should clean up our act a little more before we go off talking to people?"

"I do," agreed Orpath.

Wilton nodded and tried to think through what they had outlined during the day before.

"Well," Wilton began, taking a little time to get his thinking together. "You gave us the nuts and bolts yesterday. Maybe we should start in on some detail."

"Yes," continued Jeri, "like how are we going to eat while we're on the bridge?"

"No problem," from George, "but, let's organize getting there."

"How, and in what?" asked Wilton.

Orpath rose and began pacing from his desk to the window. "We'll need vehicles," he said. "Strong, large, maneuverable vehicles. Any ideas?"

Wilton looked over the photographs. "While you were outlining what procedures we could follow on the bridge, I thought about big, articulated moving vans."

"Good!" chimed George. "I had the same idea."

"They'd have to be armor-plated," Orpath added.

"Is it possible to 'requisition' some of the armored vehicles in the Presidio?" Wilton queried.

"You know, Ed," George answered, "I looked into that, and it would be possible. Those trucks are garaged at the bridge end of the Presidio. There's only one problem. Two days before we're set, those trucks could be moved to Nevada or Alaska. We couldn't depend on them, and anyway, we'd probably have trouble grabbing them. It's better if we control our own machinery."

Then he outlined a plan.

Articulated vans were available. Six of them could be rented, from Freuhauf or somebody. The trucks could be taken to some out-of-the-way place where it would be possible to armor them.

Orpath added that sheet steel could be picked up at the Bethlehem outlet in South San Francisco. The work would be done under a cover. "We could say we were rebuilding these trucks to handle atomic waste materials, if anyone asks what we're doing."

Just after the War, it turned out in the discussion, Orpath, hoping to turn some quick money on a highway-construction scheme, had bought a relatively large holding of land at Sebastopol, sixty miles or so north of San Francisco, for a depressed price.

The price was depressed because the Air Force had constructed a runway to be used for practice landings for all sorts of planes, across a big meadow. Its proximity to foothill country had made its continued use for a small airport unattractive.

No highway was constructed, so the added value was never realized. Although Orpath had never seen the property, he hung onto it. After some discussion, they decided to give serious consideration to the Sebastopol site. It was out-of-the-way, yet not far from Highway 101.

It was further decided that George would go to Sebastopol at the first opportunity and make preliminary arrangements.

George reported that he had found an important outlet for advanced military firepower. These vans could become as effective as tanks.

Re-rigging would take three weeks from the date of the pickup.

Orpath nodded as he saw many of his ideas included. George was a clever fellow. He had suggested six instead of four trucks.

Gas tanks and magazines would all be reinforced, or rebuilt, to make them invulnerable.

Discovery and accomplishment electrified the atmosphere.

As no better solution had been suggested, they agreed finally to garage the trucks at Sebastopol. They would have to be adapted and manned.

Wilton pointed out that the operative word was manned.' That was the next project to be discussed.

They read the news reports on Sitting Wells again, and then turned to the other ones George had found.

A name repeated in article after article was that of the militant leader of STAB: Lauris Vandingan. He was wanted by the FBI and the State of California for questioning, at least. He had always just 'not been there' when various attempts to contact him were made.

George and Orpath were in agreement that the STAB group, if these people could be found, would have much to offer as potential project partners. They would have to find Vandingan. Jeri and George would go to work on that.

In the meantime, the forest hideaway in Mill Valley would be used as front line headquarters.

Wilton would go to Stanford, as an engineer interested in writing a monograph on Bailey Willis for a prestigious engineering quarterly. He had a friend at one of them who would cover for him. His friend was willing to do this, because he felt that Wilton had been badly treated by the profession; and he readily agreed that a good, learned paper might help put things to right.

It would be old-home week, as Wilton had been

an undergrad there. His misfortune in New Jersey would not be on record, he hoped.

He took a dim view of being separated from Jeri, but he realized her potential importance as part of the STAB negotiating team.

Orpath said good night. George followed him. Wilton complained to them about his stomach — said he might sleep in tomorrow, "being as it was Sunday." After they left, he went to the bar and found himself a good bottle. He grunted something to Jeri and left. Jeri, noting the bottle, took along a container of ice. What a thoughtful wife! His 'illness' tonight and for the next twenty-four hours, if he followed his regular drinking pattern, would give her some free time on the town.

CHAPTER THIRTEEN

As Benjamin Franklin Friendly went to sleep that night, after certain connubial attentions, he thought of Wilton's face, the lady's laugh, and the little dark-haired guy collecting the bets.

"Wonder if they pay income tax," he pondered.

He was suddenly wide awake! His bureaucratic self recognized a crime before it was a crime.

Slowly, he began to fill in the background. He remembered a report and a photograph, asking the whereabouts of this engineer who was wanted for questioning. Indeed, Wilton had disappeared from view for some time after his fatal mistake.

Memory of the FBI most wanted poster, the file, the photograph, Wilton's uneven smile, his off-center eyes, flashed upon Friendly's inward eye . . .

"This man is an engineer, and he is wanted in New Jersey for questioning in connection with a homicide charge. His name was, is . . ." Ben faltered, "Wilton."

He inhaled sharply. His subconscious had come forward, as it always did, with the information he needed.

Why was Wilton here? What was he up to? What engineering expertise was he selling? Engineering? Could he be connected with the explosions?

Considering the complete devastation these explosions had delivered, somebody must have had professional engineering advice!

Friendly's mind wandered. He picked up on Jeri. Something nice happened at the top of her chest when she put her arm up to shoot her pistol. She seemed to steady her upper arm against her right breast, which sort of pushed everything into a most-delightful curve. The recoil of the pistol could be seen in a pleasant and almost-imperceptible ripple across the area of her chest just below her collarbone.

Such a person could not be all bad.

Wilton was something else. Tall, grey, handsome, brown-skinned from the sun. Perfect teeth. Eyes that seemed just a little off-center. Almost bored.

Sleep was coming fast. Tax evasion, failure to report, fraud, faulty plans, bribes, not nice, tomorrow . . . tomorrow, finally nothing.

Next morning, after breakfast and much fuss about how pretty his wife looked in a flowered kimono, he determined to try to find Wilton.

He took the telephone book and turned the yellow pages to hotels, motels. Nine million of them!

He was looking for the most swanky one. Impossible to tell from the advertising. All sounded like the Taj Mahal.

He would take a walk. Reno wasn't all that big. He would just case the casinos. Anyone making money at the shooting gallery would have a hard time leaving the slot machines alone.

Although it was Sunday morning, he found crowds of seemingly-enthusiastic people milling around everywhere.

He padded from one place to the next. Mostly, he chose to look into fancy places.

Near noon, he came upon a sumptuous building housing a fancy dress shop, a liquor store, a large bank, and one or two nondescript commercial ventures at street level. It housed the plush Regency condominiums.

At the center of all this, a dignified entryway led to a handsomely-furnished lobby. Gold lettering announced that the casino was at the third level.

Friendly accepted the emblazoned invitation. He went to the third level, and stepped into spendor such as he did not believe could exist.

He stood for several moments, taking in this scene from Sodom and Gomorrah.

Even the metallic clunking of the slot machines sounded like heaven-sent noise.

Money falling out of the machines sounded just the same. Crass, American, welcome.

He was drawn to a ten-cent machine. It was the only one in that section of legalized banditry. He put in four dimes, without realizing the speed at which they were being gobbled up. He hesitated on the fifth, said, "What the hell?" to himself, and let go.

Wheels stopped, with a nice neat pattern, and dimes of all years spewed forth.

He could afford coffee *and* apple pie.

He smiled. Pulled his winnings from the metal cup. Dropped some on the floor. He stooped to pick them up.

Rising, he looked across the row of machines, and there, eyes glued to the revolving wheels of her machine, was the breezy gal from the shooting gallery.

The wheels went clunk-clunk-clunk-snik.

Jeri said, "Shit." She glanced up and saw Friendly looking at her. She put her hand to her mouth, smiling in apology for what she had said.

He winked.

It didn't take much to get into a conversation with her.

One thing led to another. Friendly suggested a late-morning drink.

Jeri grabbed his arm as if she had at last found someone who understood her.

"Not here," she invited.

Soon Friendly had guided her to a booth in one of the darkest gin mills in Reno. It wasn't one of those six-chair booths. This was built like a 'sitting' room in a seraglio.

They ordered drinks. Jeri leaned over to unbuckle her shoe, and gave away the other half of her secrets.

Friendly was lolling against some very large cushions. Jeri seemed to think that when cushions were distributed, Friendly had received the good ones. Anyway, she came nearer to share his.

He did not object.

Soon, after quite a little to drink, they began letting their minds and hands start wandering.

"Are you married?" buzzed Friendly.

"In a manner of speaking," she whispered, "but I don't let it interfere."

And that was the last verbal exchange they had for a long time.

"Where's your husband?" Friendly seemed like the careful type.

"Upstairs at the Regency, drunk He told them that he has an upset stomach, but he's drunk."

"Them?"

"Yeah, the hyenas he's trying to help grab some dough."

"How help?"

"Oh, he's an engineer who got busted."

"Busted?"

"Christ, yes, killed a lot of people. Can't engineer anymore." She shoved the hair out of her eyes and looked over at two Friendlys.

"My, my," breathed Friendly, as he tightened his grip on Jeri's shoulder, pulling her to him.

She surrendered completely again. By now, she was well up on the couch and had cradled herself in Friendly's arms.

"I lead a very sad life," she wept. "Very lonely and, oh damn, I need a man like you."

Friendly was willing. He was begining to think she had some interesting information, as well.

"Can't engineer, huh?" he queried.

"Only for people who really aren't very nice."

"That's too bad."

"Probably dangerous, too."

"I did some engineering once," Friendly lied. "Had to use a lot of dynamite."

"Dangerous," repeated a wriggling Jeri.

"How long you going to stay here?"

"Here? Oh, I have to go back to the penthouse, too goddamned soon."

Friendly started to say something, but whatever it was was smothered by Jeri's lips, teeth, and tongue. She had somehow or other opened her blouse and guided Friendly's hand to go where it wanted to be, even if Friendly's better judgment did not agree.

He played the game until finally, Jeri fell away exhausted. Her own hands had not been idle during this last assault. Friendly tried to straighten his tie. He also tried to tidy up Jeri, who had really fallen to pieces in more ways than one. Finally, repairs were accomplished. The bill was paid. Very small, when measured against the success of the encounter.

Jeri was grateful. Almost as grateful as she would have been had she hit the Grand Slam in the casino.

"How long are you going to be here?" a kind-eyed Friendly inquired.

"They're thinking about going to some goddamned place with a Russian name in California. Sounds like Hicksville to me. Jeest, I wish you'd come too."

"Say, wouldn't that be nice," agreed Friendly. "A hick town, you say?"

"Yeah, has something to do with apples. Something 'pool.'"

"I'll try to find you."

"That'd be nice," she smiled.

And, for a moment, he thought she was ready to start in all over again.

He forestalled the next assault by opening the drape and saying, "You go first."

She did. At the door she turned. Smiled. Disappeared. Benjamin Franklin Friendly leaned against the archway for a moment, looked back at the battleground, sighed, and headed back for his hotel. His absence could be explained. What he had participated in was unexplainable.

He made a diplomatic inquiry at the desk of the Hotel Regency as to who occupied the penthouse suite. The vacant-faced girl behind the desk said, "Oh, them. He's a financier from Los Angeles, name of Orson, or something. Has some wiseacre with him, name of George." Her eyes hardened.

"Thank you, thank you very much. I wanted to sell him some rugs. I'll call him later in the day."

"Rugs, huh."

With that, and short smiles in each other's direction, she went back to sorting mail. He returned to his hotel to sort out what had tumbled into his unofficial net.

CHAPTER FOURTEEN

Monday, George and Jeri tried locating Lauris Vandingan. Obviously, he wasn't listed in any telephone directory, but the newspapers had listed the chapters of the Society. One was listed in Orange County.

Jeri and George left early the following morning by plane, anticipating an early-evening return. Orange County was the rightest of right-wing enclaves. They felt certain that they would at least find a lead there.

Locating the local chapter's headquarters, they found a strong young woman, wearing designer glasses, in charge.

They entered and introduced themselves, saying that they held ideas closely-related to STAB's; and that they'd like to be members.

"Active," said George, and he pulled out a roll of bills to pay for the initiation fees.

"I am sure the Director will be very happy to have you aboard," the glasses said. Nods and smiles. George asked whether any of the officers were available, suggesting that he might make a substantial contribution.

"Please wait a minute. There's been a meeting in progress. Maybe they're through now." She left the room through a nondescript curtain.

Several minutes passed, during which George and Jeri leafed through the pamphlets lying around, explaining the open and legal pursuits of the Society.

No square-jawed American, or even slack-jawed American, could resist STAB's common-sense program.

Articles about how the government squares itself every ten years. Articles showing that 75% of the U.S. population receives some sort of government spawned check. Articles showing that bureaucracy leads to communism. A terrible future was described, unless hundreds of thousands, indeed millions, banded together to force government down to size.

Clearly, the rich were not the only people worrying about this blight. The cost was now eating right through everybody's pocket.

"Arise, you poor dupes! Arise, you about-to-be-downtrodden! Arise, you Americans, and seize your government back into your own hands."

Heady stuff.

Evidently, hundreds of thousands of people had joined. But George had heard that membership was falling off, due to some unexplainable arrests of the more active members. He felt heaven-sent, because these people really needed some broad publicity to get their militancy back in focus.

Finally, Ms. Large-Glasses returned. "Please follow me," she invited.

They passed into a small hallway. Some stairs took them to an upper floor.

The room into which they came had obviously been used by a group of furious smokers. Every ashtray bore evidence to that.

One man remained. He was in his shirtsleeves. He could have been an accountant, or the manager of a grocery store. He was a doctor.

Introductions were made. He offered the visitors seats.

The doctor's name was Harry Hildreth Black. Dr. Black.

He said, "Nice of you to come, nice of you to want to be members, nice of you to bring money. Now, what else can you do for us?"

The remark was made lightly and without offense.

George was ready to do his work. Why waste time shuffling around?

"Yes, we want to join you, and, we hope you can join us." This was a bold head-on approach.

"In doing what?" asked Dr. Black.

"That's a long story," George started. "Believe me, our purposes are different, but by joining each other, we both stand some chance of success."

"Go on," invited the doctor.

"First of all," George said, "we'd like to speak directly to Lauris Vandingan."

"Impossible," stated the doctor

"Too bad," said George.

"You must know that every cop in the west is looking for Van." The doctor looked at a book on his desk.

"We know that, and that's why we have come here," said Jeri, taking up the pause.

Something in her voice attracted the doctor's attention. He looked at her carefully. "What do you want of Vandingan?" he asked.

Leaning forward, George said, "Like you, we want to make some heavy demands upon the government. You have been making demands, but you haven't had the clout to force the issue. Our plan has clout."

"It also seems to have money," Black said.

"Yes, we have the money and we know what to do, but we need some people."

There it was. George had put it on the table.

"People?" Black asked.

"Yes," said Jeri.

"To do what?" Black queried.

"There are five of us," George replied. "We could use at least twenty more motivated people." An understatement.

Black asked, "What do you want them to do? Picket?" And then he added, "Look here, young man. You can hire pickets for fifty bucks a day. Good, loud ones." Black was making fun.

George stayed serious. "No, not that kind of picket. These guys will be backed up by guns. Big guns. And," George paused, "well-placed dynamite."

Although he didn't say it, Black understood dynamite. "What are you going to do? Blow up the State Capitol?"

"We plan to hold a large piece of public property for ransom. We'll be paid money. If you come with us, you'll get your prisoners back. We'll all get away."

"What have you in mind?"

Jeri started to speak, but George beat her to it. "We have the guns. We have the wheels. We have the guy with us who can lay the dynamite. We need drivers, gunners, radio operators, and probably some pilots."

"Quite an order, my friend." Black smiled at him.

"Well, that's what we need. Too big an order?" He wasn't jeering, but his remark had the desired effect.

Black rose. "Excuse me a moment," he requested, and left the room.

Jeri and George exchanged looks. A shake of George's head silenced Jeri.

A moment later, Black returned and picked up Jeri's large purse. "May I?" he asked politely.

"Hey, wait a minute, Charlie," Jeri tried to retrieve her bag.

"We just don't want any guns around." He pushed his hand through her handbag like a real customs officer.

Jeri seethed.

"And you, sir?" asked Black.

"Clean," said George.

Nonetheless, Black patted George until he was satisfied that he had no gun.

"One minute, please." He left the room again.

A moment later, a man entered in a bathrobe and slippers. He had just showered. Had that nice clean smell. Broad shoulders. Short blond hair. Heavy chin. Piercing sky-blue eyes. When he spoke, it was with a good heavy voice. He was obviously well-educated.

Lauris Vandingan didn't exactly smile and he missed nothing in his quick look at each stranger.

"How did you know I was here?"

George responded, "We hoped that eventually someone would lead us to you. We didn't think we would make our contact with you so quickly."

"Maybe we're all lucky," smiled Vandingan.

"We need to speak with you."

"I heard everything you said to Dr. Black. What's your game?"

"Blackmail," George deadpanned. "For $25 million." Then he smiled.

"You seem very sure of yourself," Vandingan observed.

"We are!"

"Why do you come to me?"

"You have reason to blackmail to get your guys out of hock. Pretty important, I'd say."

"Very important."

"You probably could take the Governor hostage, and then ask for the release of your people. You'd get letters of congratulations from all over the state, telling you to keep him! None of 'em would get out."

"You say," Vandingan said.

"I do," said George. "If you want freedom for your buddies, you have to go for the jugular. We want $25 million, we go for the jugular. This is not an easy job. We thought we might kill two birds with one stone, if we could do this together."

"What do you bring in?" Vandingan asked quietly.

"Know-how, and the jugular, and a few bucks."

"Funny," smiled Vandingan.

"That's it for now. Why don't you think about it. We can shake the whole country. The government can't dump our demands. Wouldn't be able to dump yours either, once they get our message. It's a lead-pipe cinch. But we need soldiers. You have 'em."

Vandingan asked, "Where can we reach you?"

George gave him Orpath's number.

The listed telephone number of the Clubhouse was passed along by Dr. Black.

"We'll talk here. Can't promise anything, but I like the general approach." Vandingan arose, shook hands first with Jeri and then with George. He left the room. Ms. Large-Glasses showed up to take them back downstairs, and to the door.

Once outside, Jeri turned to George. "Georgie, dear," she said softly. "I have to hand it to you. I think you've just enlisted our army."

"I hope so."

Back to the airport and an hour-and-a-half wait for the Reno plane.

Once on board, Jeri put her head on George's shoulder and fell fast asleep.

George went over what had just happened. If he

hadn't been so crowded, he would have given himself a pat on the back.

He would not have been so quick at self-congratulation had he been a little mouse in the Sacramento FBI headquarters.

CHAPTER FIFTEEN

The Chief finally found time to see Friendly. Ben told him about Reno.

In deference to the Chief's youth, Ben did not go into Jeri's physical details, past the point at which he was able to buy her a few drinks to loosen up her tongue.

The Chief listened, but his expression did not show any more enthusiasm than you'd find on the face of someone at the racetrack who had just lost a sure thing.

"I don't see any connection," pontificated the Chief.

"It is a little hard," said a discouraged Friendly.

"Right," banged the Chief. "Now, Ben, here is something you *can* do. I have a complaint here from Agriculture, relative to some little water agency in Marin County. I told their man that I'd send someone over to look into the matter. You do it. San Francisco is too busy."

"OK, Chief." Friendly took the file and padded out to his own office.

His desk was covered with clippings, including the reports about Sitting Wells, Nevada.

He would go down to Marin County in the next day or so. In the meantime, he'd continue with his task of tying together dates, times, and words.

In addition to the recent Nevada report, he had, in front of him, a report on last year's explosions in Seattle. He had the news report of Vandingan's speech in Omaha of several days before that. For the moment, he brushed Nevada aside. Friendly zeroed in on Vandingan's words: 'will strangle us or be strangled,' 'death-struggle of democracy,' 'any means to save our freedom.'

Any means!

The speech had been delivered at a membership drive in a stadium in Omaha. Presence of such a group in a public place was certainly a local endorsement of free speech, at any rate.

Vandingan had left the platform when he had finished his address. One of his captains had answered questions.

At no time had it been directly suggested that any government bureau should be bombed.

The meeting had collected about $52,000 in ticket charges and contributions.

"Might be a point there," thought Friendly. "Illegal contributions."

Good God! Here was a man and an organization suspected of destroying millions of dollars of government property, and here was Friendly, thinking about whether or not these people could be prosecuted for running a contributions con game.

Friendly put the thought to one side.

He reviewed the materials connected to the bombing of the State Controller's office.

"What an idiot the Controller was," thought Friendly. "His statements were vacuous and really stupid. He didn't even know the name of one of his own department heads!"

That bombing was within the last ten days. Just preceding the explosion at the Controller's building,

Vandingan had made an impassioned address, so the press reported, to a group at Redlands; and a big Orange County contingent was reported to have trooped into the hall at the last minute, and marched to a block of seats which had been reserved for them.

Vandingan appeared and a riot of adulation swept the hall. He quieted the applause and began to speak.

He dwelt for some time on the 'strangle-or-be-strangled' theme. Then he left the hall as suddenly as he had appeared. Contributions here were said to have exceeded $167,000.

Legal?

Again, Friendly put that aspect out of his mind.

The 'strangle' theme and the ensuing explosion were beginning to form a pattern, which was what Friendly hoped would occur.

'Strangle' was the key word which excited the contributors who financed STAB's program.

Society to Abolish Bureaucracy. Indeed, quite a few public offices had been 'abolished.' Years and years of habit and regimen down the tubes!

It would take a generation to re-fit these gutted pleasure domes of bureaucratic privilege.

Benjamin Franklin Friendly did not think that Vandingan would personally surface again.

He was correct.

Full-page advertisements appeared in the *San Francisco Chronicle* and the *Oakland Tribune,* which again included the 'strangle-or-be-strangled' idea. There was a post office box number to which contributions could be sent.

"Better check that box," thought Friendly, and he made a note.

Then he wondered where the next explosion would be heard.

"But don't go too far!"

He thought about Ed Wilton and how far he had come. He'd like to see that man's travel itinerary. He'd like to know what Wilton's plans were for the next six weeks. He had a hunch that it wouldn't be going 'too far.'

CHAPTER SIXTEEN

When Jeri and George walked in from Orange County, Jeri fell into Ed's arms as if they'd been separated for six years.

Later, Orpath reported that he had located the vans. He was also in the process of having incorporation papers written. He was to be the Tri-State Coastal Moving Company. Puggo was the president of the company. Everybody laughed. Puggo didn't think it was so funny. "We'll have these papers tomorrow, and then by the end of the week, I can go over to the truck company — it's in Salt Lake City — and make the rental agreement."

Ed gave his report. He had made contact with Stanford, and after speaking to six different people, finally zeroed in on one who had known Bailey Willis.

Notwithstanding this old acquaintance, he had drawn a blank at Stanford. Bailey Willis on China, Bailey Willis on the Gobi Desert, Bailey Willis on Appalachia. Bailey Willis on Appalachia, in Russian. No Bailey Willis on the San Andreas Fault or the Golden Gate Bridge.

"It's as if there were a curtain over anything old Willis said about the bridge." Wilton was disappointed.

"We'll try newspaper files next," said Jeri.

Then George detailed the meeting with Vandingan.

Orpath became quite excited at the prospect of leading an army.

Wilton was worried about keeping the secret.

George answered, "No trouble, Ed. These are pros. There'll be no problem."

"Do they know about the bridge?" asked Wilton.

"No, they don't. When the time comes, I think only Vandingan should be told. Then, right to the last moment, we'll tell the troops something else, or nothing at all."

"These extra people will have to be housed someplace. Have you thought of that?" Wilton was like a prosecuting attorney.

"I have some ideas . . ." George snapped.

George and Orpath had dinner by themselves, as the Wiltons had decided to 'see the town.' There was a little more conversation this time. Of course, there was more to talk about.

Orpath said, "George, we have to think about the rescue plane, and we have to start planning for it."

"Easy. We'll either buy or rent a Lear jet."

"Not so easy. We'll need maintenance and a pilot. I wonder if Puggo can do it."

"Listening to how he squeaks it, he can pilot anything."

"Guess our Tri-State Coastal Company needs an airplane, too."

"Why not?" George added.

"Be nice if he could practice landing it on the bridge."

"I don't think he'll have that opportunity."

"How big is the runway at your place in Sebastopol?" George continued.

"Big. From photos I have, some of it looks like a highway going nowhere. That place used to be a training strip for the Air Force pilots. They practiced landings there with every kind of plane. I bought it a long time ago, very cheaply. It wasn't of any use to anyone."

"Pretty important now."

Orpath began thinking out loud. "We'll need at least two planes, and we'll need crews."

"I hope Vandingan has them. He seems to have everything else."

"We'll have to see."

George said, "Maybe we don't have to worry too much about the crew."

"Why not?"

"Well, maybe one other pilot. Vandingan will certainly be able to take care of a small ground crew. That ought to be enough to get us on our way."

"Where?"

"We'll have to decide that."

"I think we'll have to head for a small island in the Pacific. Even an atoll."

"Can we locate one?"

"I think so."

"Put Wilton on it."

Later in the evening, when the Wiltons returned, Orpath motioned Ed beside him near the fireplace.

"Ed," said Orpath, "we've been talking about where we go, once off the bridge." He outlined the need for a second pilot and someplace to fly, once they left Sebastopol.

"We need an island."

"I think I know the place! 500-600 miles, a little farther west than Honolulu."

"That could be good," Orpath noted.

"I worked on a little place called Gardner's Pinnacles during the War. Just the place for us. Off the travel routes, and a big airstrip in place. It may have to be cleaned up, but it can work."

"Someone better go there now and check it out," Orpath said.

"My former associate is in Honolulu now. I'd trust him. Let me call him and see what he can do."

"Good. Do it."

Ed went into the study, picked up the phone, and after some conversation with Information, he was able to get through to his friend.

Ed's friend, Bill Freeman, ran a sports fishing business, and was familiar with this general area, although he'd never been to Gardner's Pinnacles.

He was asked to charter a plane to go to Gardner's, and land, if he could. Ed told him that an account to cover expenses would be established at the First National Bank of Hawaii. Orpath would take care of that immediately.

Now they would just have to wait until Freeman could report back.

Orpath reported that he had found the steel armorplate, bought it, and ordered it shipped to the rented South San Francisco warehouse.

He had also obtained the pamphlets from Fruehauf, which described the truck interiors.

Organization for the guns and ammo was under way. Some of this would be bought in the east. Delivery would be made at three different addresses, located in Seattle, Ogden, and Bakersfield. At the right moment, all the materials would end up at the Sebastopol workshop.

All of these plans went forward without any problem, cash on the line having greased the way. But the armor-plate order hit a snag.

CHAPTER SEVENTEEN

Far away, in Washington, D.C., the order for the steel armor-plate had been picked up and given to the third clerk from the left at the Office of Strategic Services. It was Form #L-143-SSC-59. This form advised the clerk that the armor-plate had been purchased by LODALL, Inc. of South San Francisco.

Stragetic Services had an abiding interest in those private citizens or companies without government contracts purchasing materials which were normally used in the 'defense' effort.

It was the Thursday before the combined Lincoln-Washington Birthday's long weekend. The third clerk spent the day figuring out how he was going to pick up his girlfriend in Bethesda, and get to Mt. Kisco and back by Tuesday morning. That was a problem for number three, as he had no car.

He was not concentrating on government business, and by the time he hit Form #L-143-SSC-59, he could care less. It ended up at the bottom of his basket for the second time.

This delay made all the difference.

The following day, the plan suffered another setback.

Freeman called from Honolulu, reporting that he

had flown over Gardner's, and that the jungle had taken the whole island. It would take a good year's work, and a million dollars, to clear the place.

The news was passed along. George was disappointed, but Orpath just shrugged.

"Better we find this out now."

Jeri, always pleasant, wondered, "Why don't we plan to go to Puerto Vallarta? I've always wanted to see that place. Wouldn't that be fun?"

"Not fun," said George, "but a good jumping-off place. Why not?"

Orpath quickly saw that by going south, a whole new route could be opened.

"If we do that, I don't think we'll need the second plane at all," George said.

"What's the maximum distance, take-off to landing, for a Lear?" asked Orpath.

"About 2800 miles, nautical," Wilton volunteered. "That gets us to Puerto Vallarta. The Lear may be able to make it, on the second jump, to the Marquesas."

"Won't have any trouble refueling in Mexico," Orpath said. "I have friends there who'll take care of that."

Orpath continued, "Jeri," he said, "I'd like you to go with Puggo to the airport. He knows planes. Ask them to show you some Lears. We're interested in two things: maximum flight distance, and we have to know the minimum take-off and landing distances."

"Of course," George said, "we may have to use two planes. One to get off the bridge, and one to make the trip to Puerto Vallarta."

"We have to find out. Jeri, that's your job."

Jeri was looking around to find Puggo, who was not there. "We'll go this afternoon," she said.

Puggo and Jeri made their trip. A more unlikely

couple could not be described. But Puggo knew airplanes. Anyone who lived after flying B-26's the length of time he had could write the book. Puggo was such a man, only he didn't write very well, and the B-26's had become a thing of the past.

For this trip to the airport, he doffed his ill-fitting white butler's coat and put on a sweater of loud design. He hated that white coat, but Orpath thought that it was important. Around the house, it kept Puggo in his place.

When they arrived at the airport office of Lear Jet, they found a courteous middle-aged aviator salesman who quickly became smitten with Jeri's cleavage. He danced handsprings showing them the planes. He took them up, and before either one of them felt it, they'd leveled off at 18,000 feet.

In the far west distance, the hairline of the Golden Gate Bridge was discernable. Jeri smiled. Smiled more when she noticed the pilot's eyes were not on the altimeter, but on her chest. Two hits. Exhilarating!

Puggo sat back, enjoying himself. Then the pilot gave him the controls.

Puggo's face set, and away he went into the wild blue yonder. He was a kid again.

Somewhere over Red Bluff, they headed back to Reno.

The fastest, easiest ride Jeri had ever had.

Back in Reno, they sped to the penthouse.

As Puggo, with the smile of one who had 'shown them' on his face, served drinks, Jeri told the story.

The plane could land easily, if properly handled, in about 4,000 feet, maybe less. Some of the bridge floor was actually uphill. The plane could take off in less than 2,500 feet, if certain adjustments were made to the flaps. Made to order. The distance between the pylons on the bridge was 4,200 feet.

So, at last, the way was found for the escape.

Orpath breathed a sigh of relief, and drank down most of his Bombay martini. He would now set about renting or buying outright not one, but two of these planes. Puggo would go to flight school. He didn't think that was necessary, but he would go anyway.

In discussing a second pilot, it was discovered that Wilton, as a young man, had qualified for a pilot's license, of sorts. He was assigned to the schoolhouse as well.

Now, only one problem remained: the escape of the STAB members and their returned prisoners. Some viable plan had to be put together for all of them.

George figured that the prisoners would be delivered in a large Army helicopter. A troop plane. Once landed, gas levels would be checked.

The helicopter could accommodate the entire STAB party, which would be whisked away at the direction of Vandingan. Members of the group would be dropped at three way-points: Sebastopol, the beach at Stinson, and a third site near Woodlands. Fast cars, of course, would be waiting.

When the last of the group departed, they'd kiss the pilot goodbye and tell him to get lost.

With these plans in mind, it was time for a talk between Orpath and Vandigan.

Back in Washington, Form #L-143-SSC-59 had progressed, with no alarming endorsements, to the desk of a young establishment political appointee by the name of Oliver Hazard Rearpeau. He had been a product of the right Connecticut prep school, and Amherst. He wore the right suit, and he had just the right disdain for lower-level government employees, the only value of whom, in his estimation, was to add weight, by their sheer numbers, to the importance of his own office.

"What is this?" he sneered to some underling, whose name he did not know.

"Oh," said the Grade-5, "we keep track of the sales of this product."

Rearpeau was bright. They weren't going to catch him off his bureaucratic base. He appeared to nod.

"In compliance with MAG Order 5-A3674(4G)," added the Grade-5. They weren't going to catch him, either.

"Oh," was all Rearpeau could say. No commitment. Fifteen points. Then he recovered the ball. "When the Committee meets, we'll discuss this one," and into the file it went.

CHAPTER EIGHTEEN

A violent explosion rocked a large welfare office in Los Angeles.

Records by the millions were destroyed. The target had been the main Federal Welfare computer center in southern California. Checks were issued here to millions of the worthy and unworthy. It was a shrine, a Santa-Claus land. Whatever it had been, it was no more. For once, the work done was clearly understood by all, and would be missed. Grief filled the faces of petitioners as they climbed back into their shiny cars, to wend their way to the State Social Services Office where their 'other' checks were waiting.

The really impoverished made this journey by bus.

The newspapers made the most of this welfare disaster.

Orpath, in Reno, had just finished reading the reports when Vandingan called in from Carson City.

"Well, you've been a busy fellow," Orpath greeted him with uncharacteristic levity.

"Yes, busy and effective," said Vandingan easily.

"We should see each other now," said Orpath. "We have a plan that can work."

"Good."

"What's best for you?" Orpath asked.

"If you'll go to the Gibson House in Bolinas next Thursday afternoon, at one-thirty, you will be met.

Bring George and Mrs. Wilton. They know Dr. Black."

On Thursday morning, the three of them flew to San Francisco, rented a good car, and drove north. As they crossed the bridge, they slowed down. Every cable was observed. Orpath tried to visualize the plane landing and taking off. Puggo would have his work cut out. But Orpath had faith.

They crossed the bridge, went through the tunnel, and took the Stinson Beach cutoff, heading for Bolinas. They began to climb the mountain. They took the coast road. It was a clear and beautiful day. Finally, they could see the sparkling ocean. Many little boats were in view, trolling back and forth.

"Must be good fishing here," said Orpath.

George told him it was good for salmon, sometimes bass.

A few minutes later, they crested the hill. Spread before them was the small coastal town of Stinson Beach, and a large crescent sandspit.

"My God, look at that!" Orpath enthused.

Descending into the town, they saw a little restaurant near an Art Center. Jeri said, "I'm hungry. Maybe we should try to get something here." They stopped. Someone had cleverly named the place "The Sand Dollar."

Turned out that chili con carne was the 'food of the day.'

George, when he had finished, smacked his lips. "Absolutely the best," he claimed.

Then they drove on, looking for Bolinas. They rounded a little bay and missed a turn-off. It soon became apparent, from the map, that they should have turned five miles back.

They reversed the route and found their way into the unmarked town of Bolinas. They were directed to the Gibson House.

Coincidently, Friendly's trip to Marin County had been scheduled for Thursday.

As Orpath and company had done, he and his government-issue Ford rounded the hillside bend into Stinson Beach. He found the 'subject' Water District office next to the Post Office. There he was met by a serious-faced, fat old man, and a young secretary.

At Friendly's badge of authority, the girl's eyes grew very large. Here it was, happening right in front of her — the FBI . . . Dum Dah Dum Dum . . .

Friendly had called her "Ma'am," just like on TV.

The old man had something wrong with his false teeth, which made extended conversation tenuous.

Friendly opened up his enormous file.

"Agrigulture received a copy of a complaint to the FmHA in Santa Rosa," he began. "Some taxpayer here wanted to be sure his tax money was being spent properly on some work the district has undertaken with FmHA money. Neither his original correspondence, nor anything subsequent from the taxpayer, indicates fraud. But you know Agriculture. They're worried sick that there may be some taint here." He paused.

The old man started at the term 'fraud.' "Oh, there's been none of that," he croaked and clicked.

"Well, I'm glad to hear that," said Friendly. "Why do you think the taxpayer made the complaint?"

"Dunno," hissed the old man. "Probably some nut trying to get publicity."

"Could be," agreed Friendly. "People who criticize the government, particularly in small places, ought to be shown the door."

"Tried to do just that and the son-of-a-buck sued us!"

"What happened?"

"Well, before you could say 'Jack Robinson,' the

State of California come down on us and made us do all sorts of things."

"Did that satisfy the taxpayer?"

"Hell, you can't satisfy that son-of-a-buck."

"State find any fraud?"

"Hell, they didn't even look. Just come down here and told us to do about eighty-six things. We finally done 'em all and the state went away whistling." (That was something the old fellow would have a hard time doing.)

Friendly took one look at the large file he was carrying, and he realized that of its 226 pieces of paper, 223 had been ground out at various levels of public authority. Of the other three pieces of correspondence, one was the copy of the complaint; in the second, the taxpayer forwarded his telephone number; while in the third, he requested a copy of the FmHA's first letter to him. It was only a form letter, but the taxpayer had lost it. Would someone please forward a copy?

It seems that this whole deal hadn't amounted to more than $300,000.

Friendly eyed the two now-concerned bureaucrats, and realized that neither of them was capable of fraud with intent, as that took a certain amount of intelligent foresight. He quickly concluded that, while errors were highly probable, fraud was impossible.

He asked for the use of the phone. He called through to Agriculture and spoke to the official who had sent him on this journey. He explained, slowly and clearly, the obvious incapacity to perpetrate fraud of these local public servants. Then he said, "There's less than three hundred thousand mixed up in this."

"What?" cried Agriculture. "My report says $30 million! Just close that file and send it to me marked 'Personal and Urgent.'" Deep six was in process.

Ben turned to the quivering low-level bureaucrats and informed them, "Some mistake has been made. Agriculture thought $30 million was involved. Your case is closed."

The old man's teeth clicked twice. Once in relief. And a second time in recognition of what might have been. The second was sort of a sad click.

Benjamin Franklin Friendly zipped the file shut, said goodbye, and left. He'd wasted a lot of time. It was nearly one o'clock. He decided to drive to Bolinas for lunch. Having heard about the Gibson House, he headed there. He had just ordered his luncheon and was seated at a lace-curtained window showing onto the porch and driveway, when who should approach the stairway but Jeri and two others, one of whom he recognized as the black-haired bet-taker at the shooting gallery!

The other, older, pinch-faced little man he did not recognize.

As they mounted the staircase, a man rose from a chair on the porch. He advanced and inaudible introductions were made. Jeri excused herself to use the facilities while the men engaged in small talk. She passed quite near to Friendly, seated on the other side of an open door. He could smell her perfume. The Reno seraglio revisited.

When Jeri returned, perfume and all, their host went to his car in the parking lot and Friendly watched him take a briefcase from the trunk. Then the party climbed into Jeri's car. Friendly quickly marked its license number.

The young man was driving, and he pulled out of the parking area at quite a clip. Friendly rose hastily, paid his bill, and went to his car as fast as he could. He stopped just a second to jot down the number of the unused car. He noted its make and model.

When Friendly reached the highway intersection, there was no sign of the other car, and no indication as to which way Jeri and party had gone.

Black, in speaking with the younger man, whom he had called George, had not mentioned any place or direction. He had said only that they were expected.

Friendly looked in each direction. To the right: calm, quiet meadow, once part of the bay. No sound, no ripple, no suggestion.

He looked at his map and decided to go to the left. He circled up the hill past a eucalyptus grove, going as fast as the tortuous turns would permit. No sign of anyone. Then two slow-moving cars. Impatiently, he followed them to the next straight piece of roadway. Finally, he could pass, and he raced north. No trace. When he reached the crossroads at Olema, he knew he had missed his quarry.

On his car radio he called into the sheriff's office at Point Reyes Station and was referred to the county center. Once he had the sheriff on the radio, he gave the number and a description of Jeri's car. He thought the car had gone north along Highway One.

The sheriff, after one or two brief questions as to the car's description, stated that he would also alert his patrols between Mt. Tamalpais and Tam Junction. The mountain would be covered.

He was informed that the car's occupants were wanted for questioning by the FBI. Then agent Friendly headed for Sacramento.

Black, being driven at a high and dangerous rate of speed by George, directed his party through Stinson Beach, along the coast road they had just covered. After passing Muir Beach, they climbed the mountain. At a crest, they took a sharp right and descended into a valley. The valley floor had a little lake, ringed with eucalyptus trees.

To one side, they spotted an old-fashioned California house, but they did not stop.

The place was a communal living center, which had been given to this cult by the wealthy former owners. The car climbed a precipitious road, ending up on a promotory, where a great lodge-like building was nestled into the rocks. A little sign read, "Welcome to the Eagle's Nest."

It certainly looked like one.

The view demanded some attention, notwithstanding the seriousness of the visit. Appropriate things were said, and then they entered the house.

"We're here, Chief," Dr. Black called out. A door closed somewhere in the lodge, and another opened to disclose Vandingan, in his bathrobe. George and Jeri smiled. Orpath did not. Van did.

"Well, here we are," he said, after introductions.

"What a place to be!" chirped Jeri.

George was looking out the window.

Volta Orpath opened the conference with one or two perfuctory remarks, then launched into the subject of the visit.

"We have developed what we feel is a really good plan. It will take competence, but we have that, and so do you."

Vandingan said, "We hope we have. Our people in jail depend on us."

"We want to get them out," said Orpath, with his smile stretching for a fight.

"Yes," said Van.

"Vandingan," Orpath addressed the STAB Chief, "we want to get on with our job, and we are going to make full disclosure to you. You can see that this could put us at great disadvantage if you discussed it around."

"Please," said Van, "I know these things. How do you think I've survived? I've given careful thought to what your man outlined at our last meeting. We do need to make a grandstand play, and it seems to us that you have suggested a good one. Let us take it from there. For the time being, only Dr. Black and myself have any idea of what you're doing. If you choose to forget it, believe me, we're busy enough in other areas. We can't take time to worry about what no longer concerns us. Do I make myself clear?"

Orpath then asked George to proceed with the outline of the plan. The bridge, trucks, guns, dynamite, airplanes. The whole business, including the need for 'soldiers,' and what those 'soldiers' would do, and how they would escape from the bridge.

During this, Black served iced tea.

When George, assisted by Orpath, finished, Van quietly looked out the window.

"You've thought of everything, but you're not asking enough money," he concluded, after the pause, with a broad smile.

Orpath's eyes glistened in the afternoon sun.

"We can arrange that," he said.

"A very good plan, don't you agree, Black?" said Van.

"Yes, I do," answered Black.

"Well, what do we do now?" asked George.

"We study how we fit into the operating procedures. Then we look at our talent list. From this we make up our complement and its back-up." He went on, "We will do what is necessary to gain the freedom of our comrades."

He wasn't emotional. He was firm.

As Orpath looked at him, he could understand why

STAB had made so much headway against the throttling bureaucracy.

Of course, some of it was brute force. Very compelling, as the attack was against the nesting place, the spawning ground, the reports, the coffee breaks, the mail carts, the in-and-out baskets. The terrible weapons of entrenched bureaucracy.

Old and cynical as he was, Orpath was moved as he sat in the presence of this man.

Vandingan was a George Washington. Thank heavens he was here in California, and not at Valley Forge.

Dr. Black was no slouch, either. He was quiet, efficient, and effective. Doctors, in general, become quite conservative. Black had decided to do something about his conservatism.

The last piece of the plan was put in place, as Vandingan and Black began to understand the personnel requirements.

Vandingan had made two changes. First, he wanted three helicopters supplied. He would supply the pilots. He wanted army personnel on each craft, as hostages. Next, he wanted an automatic firing system for the barricading trucks to cover the escape from the bridge.

George worried that the last minutes on the bridge deck might be a little confusing. There would be confusion under any circumstances. Wilton would work with Black on the final pattern of activity.

The moment came to say goodbye. Both George and Orpath, generally without respect in such matters, felt they had been in the presence of greatness. Vandingan and Black felt they had been in the presence of some savvy operators who were capable of anything.

Jeri was mystically moved by Vandingan, and she tried to give him a very big personal kiss, while digging

93

her fingernails into his arm. He fought a losing fight to hold her off.

As they approached the car park, Dr. Black suggested they use one of Vandingan's cars.

"We'll return yours to the San Francisco airport. You may turn ours in there, too, if that is convenient."

George started to ask why but Jeri cut in with, "Boy! That's smart. Ain't no one going to catch up with us!"

They lowered themselves from the Eagle's Nest. Passed the lake and the eucalyptus trees, and regained the highway.

A frustrated Friendly was well on his way to Sacramento by this time.

CHAPTER NINETEEN

It was a miserable morning in Sacramento in more ways than one. The *Sacramento Bee* story about the bombing of the Los Angeles welfare headquarters was spread in front of Friendly.

He pulled out the advertisement which had appeared the week before in the *San Francisco Chronicle*.

He came to the realization that in each case, public statements had preceded the explosions. He was right! There was a pattern. Generally, these statements were issued at some place far from the actual explosion site.

He further noticed that 'strangle or be strangled' appeared a week or so before each explosion.

It almost looked like a signal.

Or, was it a promise?

He checked out Black's license plate. It was a rented car from Merced. He checked that out, too. The car had not been rented to Black, but to Elsie Hewitt, presumably of Solvang. Solvang produced no Elsie Hewitt. The CHP clerk said he could find no record of such a name in the driver's license computer. "Wait a minute, we do have the name, but the person is now deceased."

On an off-chance, Friendly called the Gibson House, to see if anyone knew what had happened to the car bearing Black's license plate. The manager answered. He said the car was still there. Someone had taken the tires, but otherwise everything seemed OK.

So much for Merced, Black, Hewitt, and Solvang.

After the meeting in Bolinas, George had driven Jeri and Orpath to Mill Valley, and soon they were in the hills, circling to the hideaway.

Once there, they turned on the heat to kill the damp that is ever-present, summer and winter, in these lodges.

George made a roaring fire. Jeri prepared the drinks. Orpath went over the house from top to bottom. He surveyed everything. He even walked up the drive, to the spot where the towers of the bridge could be seen.

By this time, Jeri had pulled some things out of the freezer, and dinner was started.

As they talked, they worked on their checklist. They were surprised at how much had already been accomplished.

As Orpath had not seen any of the real estate which he'd made available for the project, he suggested that early the next day he'd like to drive up to Sebastopol.

On the return to the airport, they would pass through South San Francisco, and check out the steel warehouse as well.

"I cannot tell you how impressed I am with Vandingan," Orpath mused after dinner.

"Yeah, he sure's the leader type," George followed.

"Sexy," said Jeri.

It must have started her off, because she began giving George very encouraging looks.

Orpath finally said goodnight. He took over the master suite.

"Let's take a little walk before bed," suggested Jeri.

George had to agree, and out they went.

Walking in that terrain at night was for antelope or deer. Neither George nor Jeri lasted past the first turn in the driveway.

They seized one another like a couple of magnets.

After several armholds and headlocks, George suggested that they return to the lodge. Jeri exhaled complete agreement.

As they went down the drive, they saw Orpath switch off his bedroom light.

The two soon-to-be lovers entered the porch, and then the living-room. Jeri turned off some lights, and George took care of the rest.

He led Jeri, who followed three paces in front of him (or so it seemed), to a large bedroom on the far side of the lodge and down a short flight of stairs.

The lodge was tiered against the hillside. Very convenient, as this suite was completely separate from all the other quarters.

The room was warmed. George was prepared.

Before bed, they enjoyed a leisurely communal shower, investigating each other like a couple of private detectives.

Jeri kept George on-line, which was a new thing for George.

Finally, they turned off the water while continuing one of a series of embraces.

Water dripped from their bodies, like rain down the little crevices in the hillside above the lodge.

There was not much said, as polite people do not speak with their mouths full. Lips and wandering hands provided all the conversation needed.

Then came a moment of oneness. Without benefit of towels, they sought the warmth and comfort of their nest.

Jeri kept George so busy that not once did he think of his leather belt. When he awoke the next morning, he was most surprised. Jeri was still there.

You beat the hell out of a girl, as he had in the past, and, as a rule, she doesn't stay the night. He made a mental note to try this 'way' again.

In the early morning, they kissed each other gratefully, washed, combed, and dressed for the day's occupation.

Orpath was still in his quarters. George set about the kitchen. Orange juice, coffee, toast and cornflakes were soon served up and just in time. No sooner was the table set than Orpath arrived, looking very natty, as usual.

"Off to Sebastopol!" he cried.

"First, breakfast," ordered Jeri. "Now, eat your cereal and take your vitamins."

After breakfast they closed the lodge and headed for Sebastopol. All the way to Santa Rosa, and then toward the coast.

Sebastopol is the peaceful apple center of the world. That's what the locals tell you, and God knows, there's enough cider to help them prove it! A little of that cider goes a long way.

Orpath's garage, it turned out, was part of an old cider mill. It had started as a shed next to the old mill itself. Then the long-ago owners had decided to make 'off-season' money by running a garage.

This business prospered, and they soon were doing repair work on all the trucks in the area. They did well enough to expand their original shed into a factory-like area, not far from the main road. To reach it, a turn had to be made onto a narrow, unmarked road. The entry to the cider salesroom was marked. An old, worn sign simply said, "CIDER," and pointed up a grown-over driveway.

Orpath was concerned about how the large trucks would negotiate these paths.

George said, "Not to worry." He explained that

there was a second driveway, which would permit easy entry, on the other side of the property.

They surveyed what had been accomplished in the garage area.

George had managed to find a mechanic who was willing to go 'upcountry' to install a full garage service.

He had developed a fine-metal working area, equipped for cutting and welding, in addition to ordinary garage equipment. Orpath smiled, or tried to, as only a person can who sees his money well-spent.

"Good," he said.

The workman was pleased when he saw they approved of his work. George gave him a twenty-dollar bill.

This fellow, fresh from the penitentiary, was glad to be employed, and he was not talking. He was told not to.

Orpath noticed a campsite near the work area. "Could take care of twelve people there," he observed.

On the other side of the ridge was the landing field. 4,000 feet of it, some of which was not cleared. With minimum effort, that would take three days. George asked the mechanic to find some locals for the job.

It was quite warm. George observed, "The heat here is awful. But our people won't be here that long anyway."

They drove out the back way. There was plenty of room to turn, and no overhead obstructions.

They headed for South San Francisco to see the warehouse.

Going over the bridge, Orpath could visualize the excitement of those final moments on the bridge deck.

He didn't visualize all of the excitement, nor did he visualize what 'friends' he had in Washington.

CHAPTER TWENTY

In the nation's capital Rearpeau was having an evening meeting with his Committee. It adds prestige to hold meetings in the evening. Shows you take your responsibilities seriously. Also, it gives an excuse to cover some later-evening cavorting. Rearpeau needed no excuse, as he was ummarried. However, his fellow Committee members stood in need, and Rearpeau was happy enough to oblige.

Much of the business was speedily dispatched, resulting in a varying degree of economic misery to be meted out over the country the following day.

Then, a now-battered file, stemming from Form #L-143-SSC-59, was produced. The file now had one hundred and seventy-three pages of reports, from every Agency except Fish and Game. No one seemed unduly disturbed about this purchase.

As Rearpeau looked at it, his heart filled with such pride that such a small problem could become so prolix, and in such a short time!

"Has the FBI seen this?" Rearpeau demanded casually.

"I think not," said Committee member Number 2, being paid overtime. "I do not see its name on the buck slip."

Some Agency other than Fish and Game had been neglected. Rearpeau saw release from immediate decision. "Send it along to them. It involves armor metal. Someone may be trying to bullet-proof Mafia property."

A blow struck for freedom!

The big thing, of course, was that the file was somebody else's baby now.

It was duly enveloped and addressed. Eventually, a messenger would come and take it to the central distribution point.

What Rearpeau did not know was that, in the caverns of the FBI, there existed an eager young agent who for weeks had been starved for activity; he was so starved, actually, that he thought that unless he had something to do soon, he'd be marked 'expendable' or 'surplus.' He did keep marvelously clean wastebaskets during this period, however.

Help was on its way.

The FBI agent-in-waiting for the Form #L-143-SSC-59 was Tom Dodds. He was no Benjamin Franklin Friendly. He was an accountant. He had been born in the small town of Mohall, North Dakota, a town of tough northmen. That makes for liberty. People just don't step on you when there's any chance that they may lose their right foot.

Well, young Tom Dodds, of the square jaw, was just what everyone thought Washington needed. That is, everyone but the people who make Washington tick. Not much use for square jaws in those precincts.

The messenger delivery of the burgeoning file was made to young Dodd's office. His heart leapt. There would be a full wastebasket tonight!

Dodd's boss, though no slack-jaw, was not a really busy person either. But he was different from Tom. He liked being not busy. He was from the South.

Tom took him the envelope containing Form #L-143-SSC-59. He looked dismayed at its girth.

"Tom boy, you handle thet."

"Thet" was enough for Tom. He was off and running.

When a bureaucrat wants to apply himself, there is no length to which he will not go in the exercise. All young Dodds needed to find was one questionable item.

Now, bear in mind that thirty-two agencies had passed on this meager form, and swelled its unintelligible beginnings to greatness. This made little impression on Tom Dodds. He seized it. Read every word. His eyes dimmed, and just as he began to fall asleep, the Lord's finger pointed to a hole in the report. He looked twice.

He gasped. It was true. The armor steel had been sold and delivered without complying with Section B-149A! No yellow slip had been issued! Aha!

Someone would pay for this!

Those stupes in the other agencies! This was criminal neglect. While this report was only 173 pages long, it should have been 480 pages, most of it complaints against intra-office inefficiency.

Unaware that a new approach was being made to the FBI in Washington, Benjamin Franklin Friendly continued his painstaking labors in Sacramento.

CHAPTER TWENTY-ONE

George drove Orpath and Jeri to the warehouse in South San Francisco. The steel had already been delivered. The old warehouseman could hardly see. No problem, as he put in a full eight hours doing almost nothing requiring close focus. Orpath, noting this shaky situation, immediately ordered everything removed to Sebastopol. After a few phone calls he, Jeri and George returned to Reno.

As if no trips, no excitement, no energy had been spent, Orpath called an early-morning meeting right after breakfast the next day.

Wilton had returned. Puggo was there. He and Wilton were becoming experts on the Lear Jet. They argued about the altitude at which the escape flight would be flown. Wilton wanted to fly at 35,000 feet. Puggo insisted on flying close to the water, over the border, and straight to Puerto Vallarta.

Wilton, furthermore, had figured out what was needed to get to the Marquesas, although no particular island had been chosen.

"Now, I've come to another conclusion," he said. "I think it's too hard to work with gold all around. We are asking for $25 million. At $500 per ounce, that's about two and a half tons. That's an impossible weight." Wilton was very serious. Why it had not occurred to him before was not explained. After all, he was the engineer.

Although Orpath had wondered about the weight, he had not gone through the numbers.

There was indeed another way to transfer gold. It would take longer, but it could be done, as a truck could be set up with a trans-Atlantic radio telephone.

"Orpath, do you have a Swiss banking connection?" Wilton asked.

"Of course."

"Do you speak to your agent by phone frequently enough to recognize his voice?"

"Well, not frequently, but I'd recognize his voice if I heard it."

"Good. Then here's what you must do."

Orpath bridled. He did not like anyone telling him what he *must* do, even if he would have done it anyway.

"Well," said a sour Orpath.

Wilton enumerated.

"One, we will need three more accounts. George, Puggo, Jeri and myself, and we will need numbers. Two, these accounts must be established to receive telephone transfers from the government's gold account."

"Yes," said Orpath.

"We demand a transfer of twenty million dollars in gold by the United States Treasury to these accounts," Wilton continued. "Three, once we are advised by the bank that the credit is established, we will leave. If it is not, we will blow the bridge — after we leave, of course."

"Of course."

"That is not all."

"Yes."

"The State of California must contribute, too. We tell them to deliver $5 million in bearer instruments,

104

in $10 thousand denominations. And $250,000 in cash."

"Is that all?"

"I think that's about all we will be able to carry."

"Well, well," mouthed Orpath, making a chapel with his fingers.

"The Swiss accounts can be arranged and that will take care of most of the money. The rest will be a convenience," Wilton said. Orpath nodded.

Changing the subject, Wilton then discussed plans, based on the engineering designs he'd found at the public library.

He told everyone that he was studying the clever stress-balancing principles which had been developed by Strauss, the bridge engineer.

"You know," he said, "I pretend that I'm Strauss, going over my own plans, looking for the weak link."

"It's there," he added, "and I'll find it."

"Bravo, Ed!" said Orpath, with confidence.

"In the meantime, I'm also becoming a good pilot. When we finally take over those two planes, Puggo and I are going to race to Alaska and back."

All laughed, even Puggo, whose laugh was more peculiar than his manner of talking.

Orpath was concerned about the deployment of their 'troops.'

"Let's start from the bridge and work backward."

"On the bridge, what technical jobs do they have to do?" George asked.

Wilton came forward.

"They'll have to work with me in placing the dyna-mite."

George added, "They'll have to man the artillery and run the guard detail."

Wilton said, "I'll need a couple of personnel carriers and some motor-bikes. We'll have two communication centers. We'll start out with the one on the San Francisco side, but we'll have all the same equipment at the Marin end. I have to check the effect of the mountain on reception."

Orpath listened carefully.

"I'm wondering," he suggested, "if we should have a middle barrier, as a sort of fall-back position."

"I don't think so," said Wilton. "It would block the runway function of the bridge, and besides, if the occasion arose for a fall-back, we'd probably blow the bridge anyway. Sad, but true. So, we're in a make-it-or-not situation. There really is no fall-back position to take."

"We'll be there only a relatively short time," hoped Orpath. "You are right. We just have to make it. We must try not to get wet."

Wilton said he'd have a work schedule made up which would peg each job.

"We may have to change it here and there, depending on what comes up, but at least we'll know the general plan."

Orpath was still thinking of the payoff.

A large advertisement from the *Seattle Times* was flagged for Friendly's attention.

Again! He wondered, "Where now?" Illegal contributions did not occur to him this time.

Within three days, 'where now?' was Denver!

Again, the newspapers had a hell of a time describing the work product of the once-active building. It wasn't secret work. It just wasn't understood by the people who worked there, or by any other government bureau in the neighborhood.

Imagine! This last building was in for a bare-bones budget of $454 million a year, and employed 9,246 employees, not one of whom was killed or injured.

However their desk space was a terrible mess. A whole series of terrible messes is more like it.

The building itself had been leveled, pinning underneath its fallen beams the entire federal-government motor pool for the Denver district!

Some federal fat cats were seen driving their own cars! Others were seen in taxicabs. Very few rode the buses.

On the foggy shores of the Potomac, young Tom Dodds was able to procure orders to run an investigation in San Francisco. Ordinarily, this would have been bucked to the San Francisco office, but in view of the time available to Dodds, it was decided to send him. He was to check in, of course, with that overworked San Francisco office. He packed his bag.

CHAPTER TWENTY-TWO

George felt that final plans to bring in STAB should be undertaken. Supplying the labor for work on the trucks was the first priority. Indeed, drivers had to be supplied to get the trucks from Salt Lake City to Sebastopol. Wilton was asked to start working with Dr. Black.

The armament had to be secured. Most of this would move at night.

Orpath had arranged for an east-coast operator to pick up an armaments order in a coffin-manufacturer's truck, and head west. The other loads could also be disguised.

George contacted Vandingan.

A meeting was arranged, and Vandingan showed up at the penthouse. He looked like the typical small-time gambler from Sioux City. He had a moustache and rimless glasses. There were sixteen other men downstairs who looked just like him. He was quite relaxed for a person who'd just blown up a federal office center.

Vandingan was very pleased. He allowed himself one scotch and soda.

Dr. Black was expected to arrive, as well as another trusted aide in charge of personnel.

Ed Wilton came in from his Lear jet lesson, and was introduced. Puggo also arrived from the garage.

As George and Jeri materialized, it was decided to have an early dinner, and then to go to work on the details. Vandigan was given the other guest suite, and he went there to shower and nap.

Dr. Black arrived with a Mr. Wallace Shoppe, who, it turned out, possessed complete recall. His eyes competed with Orpath's, small and sharp. He had no smile at all. Wilton thought that this fellow must be very good at something. It was obvious he had not been chosen for his social graces.

Before the evening progressed very far, he had produced. He staffed the 'army' with 156 people.

He had already worked out the living accomodation requirements. He'd made a study of Stinson Beach, Sausalito, Olema, and Sebastopol.

A 'school' had been arranged in a large house in Stinson Beach on Seadrift which was owned by some accomodating people named Burret.

This arrangement had not been easy. Seadrift Beach houses were not supposed to be rented for anything but fun and money. However, the lateness of the season, the money, and the fact that this was an educational effort made the difference. This was to be a sort of 'think-tank' for young engineering types. OK, this once.

As a matter of fact, these 'students' would be the nucleus of Wilton's demolition team.

The big green house had enough space for dummy structures to be positioned for purposes of practice and understanding.

While Shoppe was looking at the place, a nice neighbor lady brought some homemade bread, as a sort of welcome wagon. She was treated very politely, and escorted to the driveway entrance.

A similar set-up had to be established at Sebastopol, but for a different type of personnel — this time, top sheet-metal workers. This group was evenly divided between male and female. It had been discovered, during World War II, that women could rivet just as well as men. A song, now forgotten, had been written about Rosie the Riveter.

Temporary bunkhouses were planned, made of good camping equipment.

Under Shoppe's direction, drivers were being sent to Salt Lake City. They would have the big trucks undercover at the cider mill in Sebastopol within the next two days.

Six helicopter pilot-mechanics were on the list. Four large tankers of high-octane fuel had been ordered, and would be placed under the trees near the landing strip.

This man Shoppe had everything in line.

When his flat-toned report had been given, there was hardly anything left to talk about. That was true until the arrival of General Forest Long.

Vandingan introduced him as a top-strategy expert from one of the big oil companies, on loan to STAB.

He had been a General in the armed forces. He was doughty and he was trim. His language was very broad, and very little was said that wasn't neatly punctuated with just the right expletive . . . he cursed a lot.

He was to organize the march onto the bridge, and the placement of the barriers. He would command the defense perimeters.

He gave a clipped report which resembled his salt-and-pepper moustache. There would be no fooling around. Sebastopol would become a parade ground. Calisthenics every morning. Cold showers. Baseball. Cross-country runs. Small-arms practice. It sounded as if there could be a few heart attacks. Damn it! Those who lived to get to the bridge would be in top shape.

George, who had trouble seeing how he was going to do all of this, was much relieved when it was announced that the regimen applied only to STAB personnel. Moderate exercise was prescribed for Orpath and his friends.

Long then produced a large topographical map which Puggo assisted him in taping to the mantel over the fireplace. Taking a little swagger stick, which he carried, he demonstrated how the vans would move down Highway 101 and make their bridge approach. He seemed to be participating in a fencing match with the map.

"Just holding the bridge in the first stages," he poked, "will require a good deal of protection from the surrounding mountainside. Unfortunately, the Marin tower and its abutment are not separated from the land by any water as the San Francisco tower is. Consequently, we are going to have to protect ourselves against any forces which try to gain access to the bridge by use of the tower base itself. This means we must deny access to the land surrounding the tower and the bridge ramp."

Orpath arose from his chair, stepped forward and squinted at the topographical map. "Actually," he said, "we are going to have to surround this bridge approach."

This was the conclusion which General Long had wanted to deliver himself. "You've got it," he snapped, irritated by Orpath's interruption. "We are going to have to operate with three paracommando units who will carry some rather heavy anti-aircraft armament with them. At the 350-foot level above the bridge there is an old gun emplacement. This is easily accessible to our trucks. We will move in a complete ack-ack unit. In the meantime, up here at about 800 feet, our helicopters will land some more troops and equipment and we will also land a contingent over-looking the southern mouth of the Waldo Tunnel. The fourth contingent will man the observation parking space at the entrance of the bridge. This group will command the heights above Fort Baker.

"While our men are going into their positions on these heights, some of Wilton's group will start mining the bridge approach between the observation point and the Marin Tower."

Wilton added, "Of course, while we're doing that we will also make our preliminary placement of explosives at road level on the bridge. This much of the operation will take one hour, thirty-six minutes from the time we arrive."

George, who had investigated the service road underneath the bridge, riffled through the photographs until he came to one showing a narrowing of the road. It showed the Bay. Then he demonstrated how a boat from Sausalito could make a landing.

"This is Lime Point," he explained, "a spot at which a boat landing could be made. I think the road here should be blown out to make it much more difficult for the opposition to approach the bridge abutment."

Long gave George a look which would have reduced any sergeant to buck private.

"We anticipate that our detail will have that road under observation and that no landing there could succeed."

George countered, "I think some thought should be given to my idea anyway, because a landing party could scale that cliff and get onto the underpinnings of the bridge roadway without too much difficulty."

"O.K." snapped Long. "Now, as to Fort Baker, these people will not be armed," he explained, "and we can evacuate them, forcing them to leave by the small road to Sausalito."

It became apparent during this discussion that protection of the vans holding the north tower was going to be a major military operation. Wilton observed, "The control of these headlands during the first few hours is going to be very important. However, once we get our dynamite in place, the threat of losing the whole bridge will force the government to think twice before they try to attack us."

Vandingan liked the idea of having the ack-ack protection in the old gun emplacement.

He turned to Wilton and said, "It seems to me that this area between the bridge abutment and the cliff ought to be booby trapped."

"Yes," said Wilton, "General Long and I have made plans to do just that. Our trucks for this purpose will leave the convoy on the north side of Sausalito and proceed to the service road which takes us to Lime Point."

The game plan had taken on the dimension of an invasion.

Orpath and George were left to work out the negotiating tactics with Vandingan.

Ed Wilton was engineer in charge of demolition, of course. In that area, he was in command.

Orpath found it hard to believe that a group could be so dedicated. This was easily understood. Orpath's existence and success had flaunted the law and the American system. He made a mockery of it and he waxed rich. Through loopholes, well-placed political friends, and payoffs, Orpath had made the system work for him.

How could he possibly understand these patriots?

How could he understand anyone willing to take to the battlefield to make American government work the way it should?

Talk about strange bedfellows!

But they all agreed that no piece of public property in the United States could better suit the aims of these two groups: freedom for their friends motivating the STAB leadership; plain, ordinary greed motivating Orpath and his crew.

CHAPTER TWENTY-THREE

Notes on Jeri's conversation in Reno were laid out on Friendly's desk.

The 'Russian' name ending in 'pool,' where apples were the big thing, was easily recognized as Sebastopol.

Why would any group of crooks go there? To do anything? To hide? To hide something? To hide what was being done!

What would be done that should be hidden? That was a good question, and a point which should not be forgotton. Friendly jotted these notes. He really wanted to corner Wilton.

He went to see the Chief.

"Chief," said Friendly when they were alone and seated, "I think I should go back to Reno and check the test-site that was bombed. Something new may have occurred to one of those employees."

"What happened in Stinson Beach?" said the Chief. He had the memory of a St. Bernard dog.

"No problem," responded Friendly. "The Ag guys thought someone was playing around with $30,-000,000. When they found out it was only $300,000, they weren't interested. I understand the complaining taxpayer is very upset, but Ag isn't going to do anything."

"You have a little time now?" the Chief raised his eyebrow.

"I could spare two days."

"OK. Make them count. Need any help?"

"Well, I may, but I'll call."

"OK. Send Mildred in, will you?"

Mildred was just what the Chief needed. Her dictation was slow. Her typing was not much either. Her bookkeeping was nonexistent. But, she wore spike heels and a see-through blouse. The Chief could afford to take his time dictating.

Friendly was on his way to Reno.

After an uneventful but tiring ride, he pulled into Reno about 9:30 that evening. He went to the hotel at which he and Honey had stayed on the previous visit.

He was tired. He wanted to go over to the gold-plated casino, but he thought he'd just get a good night's sleep.

The emergency phone number was in his pocket. This probably could bring the local police help, if not the FBI.

He'd see in the morning what more would be needed.

He planned to pick up Wilton for questioning. He figured that he had legitimate grounds for this, as Ed was not supposed to be passing out engineering advice, professional or otherwise.

What was he doing here? Where had he come from? Where was he going? Who was he seeing? Who was this man in whose apartment Wilton and his wife were living? Was he an employer? An old friend? For how long, and from where?

Somewhere in this line of questioning, the shadow would give way to light.

A sandwich, a shower, and a good night's sleep.

Maybe he'd get help in the morning. Maybe not. He headed for his shower, just as Orpath, in his penthouse, suggested a finishing touch to George and the others.

"The mechanical side of the project is complete," he smiled tightly, "even our escape," he coughed, "eh . . . departure." He did not like to use the word 'escape' as he felt that getting away was part of the offensive act.

"We have about three weeks, I gather, before B-day."

"Give or take a day or two," Wilton agreed.

"Up until now we've done nothing illegal." Orpath looked like the good little boy.

"Unless of course, you don't recognize conspiracy to steal public property as a crime," laughed George.

"Well, I mean, we're not attached to anything yet," Orpath spoke to his point. "Now, I think it would be sensible if we all left the country."

"That would certainly be a good alibi," smiled Wilton.

"How could you do the bridge project if you weren't here?" asked Jeri.

"Oh, we'll be here," Orpath answered with a small twinkle in his eye. "But they won't *know* we're here."

"Sounds like something from the Magic Castle," George added.

"Well, it is, kind of," Orpath agreed. "You remember everyone took care of getting a valid passport?"

"Yes," said Jeri, "and I hated my photograph."

"Well," announced Orpath, "I had 'duplicate' passports made up."

"You what?" exclaimed Wilton.

"I had an extra made for each of you, complete with exit stamp, in a different name." Orpath tried not to smile. He continued. "I didn't know exactly how we were going to operate, but my experience has shown that multiple ID's can be useful."

"I'll be damned," said George.

"Well, I want to be the Queen of Sheba," laughed Jeri.

"Baby, you already are!" George whispered.

"What's that?" Wilton leaned forward.

"I said, 'that's going pretty far,'" explained George.

"Umm, yes," said Wilton.

Orpath took over. "Each of you has two passports. My suggestion now is that we all leave the good old U.S.A. on passport #1, and return on the pre-exit stamped passport #2."

"It'll give us a paid vacation, Ed. We haven't really had one since . . ." and she nearly mentioned the great unhappiness in Wilton's life. "Anyway, it'll be a nice rest," said Jeri.

"Yes, nice," agreed Wilton.

George, with some idea of what rest was for Jeri, nearly laughed out loud.

"We can go to Mexico." Orpath was planning. "It won't make any difference where you come in with passport #2."

"Volta, this is a hell of an idea," George conceded.

"We'll close this place," Orpath stated. "And we'll leave at different times. We'll meet at the Mill Valley spot in ten days."

Wilton thought for a moment. "I have some bonding problems with the smaller explosives. I'll get my supervisors working on it at Stinson Beach. Let them try to pull the problem together, then I'll get back there probably within the week."

"Oh, no you don't!" yelled Jeri. "I want my full ten days!"

118

Orpath said, "Well, you folks will have to settle that. I am leaving in the morning with Puggo. He ought to look over possible landing sites."

George looked sad. "That leaves poor me."

Orpath said, "No, it doesn't. You go to Puerto Vallarta and see my contacts, so that we can let them know that we're coming." He added, "I'll give you my friends' names. I'm going to the Marquesas and find us a comfortable place to stay for a little while."

The business lights went out for the last time at the penthouse.

Early the next morning, everyone was ready to go.

CHAPTER TWENTY-FOUR

Friendly slept until seven-thirty, arose, relieved himself, took his bath, shaved, ordered breakfast, and gave consideration to the manner in which he would proceed. He decided to go it on his own.

His first task would be to go to the Federal District Court and get the Judge to provide him with a warrant so that he could collar Wilton.

He reached the courthouse and found that one Judge was sitting. When he arrived at the Judge's Chambers, the secretary asked him to wait until the Judge could leave the bench for a moment. Meanwhile, she prepared the order, which would give Friendly his authority.

The Judge finally came back to his chambers shortly before noon. He signed the order, wishing Friendly luck.

Somewhat frustrated, Friendly began the short walk to the hotel of the golden casino.

Reaching the lobby, he asked at the desk for Mr. Wilton in the penthouse.

"Mr. Wilton has left," the clerk said.

"For how long?" asked Friendly.

"I don't know."

"I'll speak with Mrs. Wilton."

"She went with him."

"When will they return?"

"They've all checked out. The Wiltons about an hour and a half ago."

Friendly didn't even say "thank you." He bolted out the door and grabbed a cab.

"Get me to the airport, pronto," he ordered, "FBI."

The cab driver was probably a weekend racing enthusiast. On this ride, he picked up some weekday practice.

Friendly threw him a $20 bill and ran for the terminal entrance.

He checked every gate. At some, people were waiting. He scanned every face. At others, people had boarded the plane and stragglers were getting their boarding passes. Waving his FBI card, he waded on to the plane, looked at everybody, and left for the next gate. One plane had just taken off. Families of the departed were turning their backs to leave. At this place, Friendly thought he picked up the scent of Mrs. Wilton's perfume. That plane was flying to Dallas and New Orleans.

The whiff of perfume was enough for him. With one look at the trail of the departing plane he ran to the police headquarters at the airport Administration Center. Here he gave a description of Wilton, and asked that he be detained at Dallas or New Orleans.

The police on duty were very efficient. Yes, they would put through a hold and notify Friendly at his hotel.

There was nothing more to do. He went back to his hotel, arriving there at four o'clock.

He had seen nearly everyone who had left Reno between 12:30 and 2:15 on that particular day. He was exhausted.

At six-thirty, a call came through that the Wiltons

had not landed at Dallas. At nine-thirty they had not disembarked at New Orleans. Friendly's heart sank.

He lay down and closed his eyes for just one second; then sat bolt upright. Had the plane stopped at Houston?

He called. It had. He cried out with rage.

As Orpath's team, and a frustrated Friendly, left Reno, G-man Tom Dodds arrived in San Francisco. He reported immediately to the San Francisco District Office. The man to whom he was to report was out to lunch. Or, so a secretary thought. When he didn't return, the story was that he had gone to the funeral of some local policeman who died in bed at the age of 87. No contact was made that day.

Dodds returned early the next morning to meet a rather unsteady agent, who seemed overcome by grief. "The coastal provinces," thought Tom. "People take things really seriously here."

He told the misty-eyed agent about his assignment. The man gave him an airy wave of his hand and told him to go to it, use his office, use his secretary, use his in-and-out basket.

What generous courtesy!

Dodds began his search.

The steel company did not have trouble identifying the buyer. It shouldn't have had any trouble — Form #L-143-SSC-59 included a copy of the order.

But there the trail seemed to end. The steel had been picked up and signed for, and that was the end of the steel company's interest, since the order had been paid for.

Who signed the receipt?

That bore fruit. It was a local handler.

The handler led Dodds to the South San Francisco warehouse.

The old, nearly-blind guard said, "Yes, sure, but they're all gone now."

"Where?"

"Dunno. Just come with a couple of trucks, picked the stuff up and left."

"What kind of trucks?"

"Big ones."

Dodds asked a few more FBI-sounding, but fruitless, questions and then left in search of the proverbial needle.

CHAPTER TWENTY-FIVE

Wilton and his wife had just vanished. This bothered Friendly.

Ben looked at his notes. Sebastopol. Why not go over there and take a look around? The Wiltons, using Houston as a blind, may have gone into Mexico in a rented car, then backtracked to Sebastopol or someplace, even Stinson Beach. He bet on Sebastopol.

Maybe some bartender would remember Jeri, or her drinking companion.

He'd take a chance. The weekend was coming up, and he would take a little trip to the apple country.

He set off early Saturday morning, alone. His wife's sister had shown up at the last minute, and the two of them had chosen not to accompany Ben to Sebastopol.

As he drove along, he wondered what he'd be looking for. If he could only find Wilton! He had armed himself with a California warrant, so that he'd not have trouble on that score.

"What's the sense of bird-dogging this place?" he asked himself. "Maybe it would be a better idea to rent a plane, and have the pilot fly over the territory. Something might jump out of the ground pattern."

He went to the small-planes airport at Santa Rosa, where he found himself a plane and a pilot.

The pilot knew the country very well, and agreed to fly a search pattern.

Soon they were 2,500 feet over the Russian River. The pilot pointed out the Bohemian Grove. It looked like just another forest to Friendly.

They located Sebastopol itself, surrounded by a regular pattern of orchards. Not very revealing.

At last they flew over a ridge, and Friendly spotted Orpath's landing strip.

"What's that?" he yelled at the pilot.

"An old landing strip, used in World War II. It's been cleaned up — must be going to open it for drag racing again."

"Let's look at it."

The pilot spiralled.

"Can we land?"

"I think so."

"Let's."

The plane landed. The runway was rough, but as the pilot had said, it had been recenty cleared.

The pilot taxied the plane to a stop.

Friendly looked around, and then he saw them: six enormous articulated moving vans.

"Can we get over there?" He pointed to the trees which covered the vehicles from the air.

"Sure."

As they taxied to the trucks, they noticed men at work.

When the plane came to a standstill, Friendly climbed out and started to walk toward the caravan.

He had been spotted, and a bristling man in boots came toward him.

"Hi," waved Friendly.

When the man was close to him, Friendly was impressed by his crisp little moustache.

The man was not the welcoming sort. That, Friendly recognized immediately.

"Your landing field?" he queried.

"In a way. What do you want?"

"I just saw it from the air, and the pilot said he could land. And so, we did. Hey, what are all those moving vans doing?"

"We're fixing them."

"Kind of a funny place to be fixing anything. What are you doing to them?"

The man made no move inviting Friendly to make an inspection.

"These trucks are being prepared for service at San Onofre. They are to carry atomic waste."

"Well, well," from Friendly.

"Yep. Didn't want to do the work on the site because of the goddamn demonstrators. My employees are non-union and I'd have picket troubles."

"Makes sense," offered Friendly.

"Yeah. We're already behind schedule."

Just then a machine made a loud whining noise, which ended in a crunch and line of profanity.

A man came out of the nearest truck and yelled to the crisp moustache, "Boss, can you come here a minute?"

"Goddamit!" said the little man. "I have to make all the goddamned decisions. Anything else I can do for you?"

"Got any cider?"

"Nope. One glass of that stuff and my whole goddamned crew would have the drizzlies. Sorry."

He looked as if he expected Friendly to at least ask for directions, but Friendly just said, "Thanks" and went back to the airplane.

"Atomic waste," he thought to himself. "How the hell are they going to handle that one?"

He climbed back into the plane. Made some remark to the pilot about the heat and how good the breeze would feel at 2000 feet.

They took off. As they did, Friendly noticed the garage site, which he had missed when they landed.

"Have to take your hat off to American ingenuity," he thought. Those 'damned' pickets hadn't slowed this job down, at least.

The end of the day was closing in when they returned to Santa Rosa.

Now, he would drive into Sebastopol and visit a few bars.

He could have saved his time. No one knew anyone like Wilton, but many would have liked to have known Mrs. Wilton.

"Bring her around sometime," said one fellow, who was already getting excited just from Friendly's description of her.

Sebastopol: zero. Except that those big trucks would be ready before San Onofre.

Friendly drove back to Sacramento for a late dinner with his wife and sister-in-law.

CHAPTER TWENTY-SIX

George flew to Los Angeles, and then directly to Puerto Vallarta.

It did not take him long to locate Orpath's contact.

Certain financial arrangements were made, and all assurances were provided that the plane would be well taken care of when it returned.

An address and call number were provided, and after six 'hasta la vistas,' George was back on the plane again, with passport #2 and girlfriend #1.

She had already been seated on the flight headed for Chicago. Two drinks and the pick-up was made. Three, and there was a re-arrangement of space. By the time dinner had been served, these two were old chums. They decided they would like to see St. Louis. Before they landed in Atlanta, the steward had re-written their tickets and told them of a gem of a hotel, small and perfect. This hotel became their home away from home, wherever that was, for the next eight days and nights.

George played it straight and the girl couldn't leave him alone. By this time, George would have been happy with suspenders. He'd even bought himself a decorative belt made of elastic.

Orpath and Puggo flew from San Francisco to Mexico City, and then on passport #2, they flew to the Marquesas.

Orpath had one old friend there whom he hoped was still alive. The fellow was a Frenchman to whom Paris was no longer available.

He was alive and at liberty. His name was Hercule Brochand.

They had several long talks, and finally Brochand came back with some good news. He had found an island which had been used for emergency landings by aircraft separated from carriers during the World War II excitement.

It was located about 300 miles from where they were. The island was not inhabited. Probably good water supply.

Could they take a look? Yes, he would arrange the plane.

Next day, with Puggo next to the pilot, they took off. The pilot plotted the island and figured eighty minutes. On the nose, the island dutifully appeared.

Puggo checked the map. The pilot circled. The airstrip could be easily seen.

The island was little less than a mile long, and the airstrip ran almost the whole length of the island.

"Can you land?"

"Pas de problem."

The sensible question should have been, "If you land, can you get off again?" Probably the same answer, "Pas de problem."

They landed.

The pilot taxied up and down the strip twice.

Orpath, with eagle eyes, located a place to hide the plane.

They all got out.

Yes, there was water and cover. Very good.

"Who owns this?"

"God."

"Alone?"

129

"Yes."

Very good. No one would bother them. The group could stay a week, a month. Very good. But bring food.

Puggo made some notes. He had brought the official navigation map and he marked it.

If worse came to worst, he'd have to sight the Grand Marquesas and then find this island. Hopefully, they'd get here in the daytime.

"A little short, the runway," he thought. "Well, some trick flying will bring us in. Pas de problem."

They paid off Brochand and the pilot and returned to Mexico. Then with passport #2, they crossed the border near San Diego.

Neither Orpath nor Puggo were 'in' the United States. That is, as far as Customs and Immigration were concerned.

They flew to San Francisco, hired a car, and drove to Mill Valley.

Before going to the hideaway, they stopped at a grocery store and bought some supplies. Then Puggo, with a little trouble, found the driveway, and they floated in.

No one else had arrived, they thought. Actually, the Wiltons had just preceded them, left their things, and then driven directly to Stinson Beach. Ed had picked up a great idea, and wanted to try it on the model.

Orpath made himself comfortable. Puggo found snug quarters and began putting an evening meal together. Just as they had made the fire, the Wiltons and George walked in, having come into the driveway at the same time.

With duty calling, and without even a goodbye to Cindy Lou or whatever her name was, George had walked out on St. Louis, gone to the airport, and found his way to the hideaway.

No sooner had they arrived than Wallace Shoppe joined them. There was some swapping of small talk which irritated Shoppe who was all business.

"Well, we are ready," he announced. "The trucks are fortresses."

"How do they move?" asked George.

"Like a dream."

On that happy note, the party broke up.

Wilton took Shoppe back to Stinson Beach to stay for the next few days, and a happy George found his way to Jeri's 'hideaway.'

Before snuggling down for the 'long winter's nap,' George ascertained that there was another exit from the suite, which would take him back directly to his own quarters in case of fire.

It was the lull before the storm.

CHAPTER TWENTY-SEVEN

The lull didn't last long.

B (for Bridge)-day and hour were set in the next meeting between Orpath and Vandingan.

Shoppe was the master cylinder of the project. That became very apparent. He was everywhere. Wilton was with him much of the time.

In going through the files of the *San Rafael Independent Journal*, Wilton had finally found the linch pin. Why Strauss or Willis had not found it remained a question. Bailey Willis had pointed to the spot without knowing how right he was.

Willis, in his crabby statement, had actually pointed to something else, but in doing so had used a term that put Wilton on the track.

Had the old professor gone one step further instead of being satisfied with the eighteen steps he had taken, he'd have discovered the simple mistake which had been overlooked by the great Strauss.

This area, through some mathematical oversight, was unbalanced. This had not been discovered since completion of the bridge, as its location received very little vibration. Had it been otherwise, Bailey Willis would have seen his prognostication come true, but for entirely different reasons than he had advanced.

Wilton and the team at Stinson went through the drill fifty times. Everyone was confident that the plan would work.

Notwithstanding the importance of this one contact

point, the drill included the placing of charges on each suspension cable, as well as going through the bridge floor above each pylon. Although the pylons were solid-looking from the outside, they were hollow. The plan called for lowering heavy charges of dynamite into each pylon.

With all of this activated, the bridge, on provocation, would literally slide into the cold waters of the Golden Gate.

Ed Wilton and his team had other problems. They had to devise an alarm system which would pick up any effort by the Army or the Coast Guard to mount the bridge.

Electronic warning devices would be used, in connection with a series of small explosives, set with photo-electric cells beamed at the vulnerable target areas.

The explosion would be severe enough to give the defenders warning and give serious concern to the attackers.

The trucks, now under the command of General Forrest Long, would provide superior anti-aircraft cover, as well as cannon cover of the approaches. The mountain commando units would be depended upon for early support.

Orpath, meanwhile, was fine-honing the demand structure.

He would demand cash and bearer instruments.

The total package could now exceed $25,000,000, and be easily transportable.

While he was in the Marquesas, he had made banking arrangements for the bearer bonds. U.S. paper, in these places, was as good as gold.

This idea pleased Orpath.

He'd deposit the instruments in the Bank of France. Then, he would borrow against them, to provide a cash account. Normally, a loan this size would raise eyebrows. But with the large sums being invested in the South Pacific for hotels and other real estate developments, no one would look twice.

Once the proceeds of the loan were banked, Orpath would make deposits to six Swiss accounts. One for each of his partners, and two for himself.

The cash would be divided on the spot.

Well, there it was. The best-laid plan of mouse and man.

All set to go awry.

Meanwhile, Dodds wasted time in San Jose, thinking it was an important manufacturing area. This was true, but it produced no clue for him. He checked Oakland, again with the same results. One of the people he had pestered suggested he go up to Santa Rosa, more to get rid of him than to help him. It worked.

He went to Santa Rosa. He began to check metal companies. None provided a lead. At last! In Petaluma: a tool salesman who'd delivered a pre-paid order for some cutting tools to a party he did not know.

They were heavy-duty cutting tools. Paydirt? Dodds leapt for joy in anticipation. He knew he was now in the right territory. He knew in his heart that he'd get his yellow form filled out correctly. He would assess a stiff penalty for failure to file it in a timely fashion and according to regulations.

In not-so-far-away Sacramento, the 'other' FBI agent, Benjamin Franklin Friendly, was horrified to receive another large advertisement. This time from the *L.A. Times*. 'Our golden opportunity is at hand,' 'strangle or be strangled,' 'gateway to freedom,' 'help!'

By God! They were going to do it again. Friendly buzzed his Chief. "May I come up?"

"Give me fifteen minutes."

The fifteen minutes was more like an hour. The Chief was being interviewed. One word led to another, and finally, he fell hook, line, and sinker for the blonde TV gal making the tape. He became expansive, even voluble.

Finally, it was over. Friendly was hot around the collar.

"OK, Ben, what is it?"

Ben then outlined all that he had found, and what he thought of the combination of events. He then pointed to the last ad.

The Chief looked at the mass of material on his desk.

"Well, what do you know?" he said, with expression.

"I think something big is about to happen," came firmly from Friendly.

"I'll check the Governor's office and get back to you."

Friendly left. With bad feelings. He went back to his office and sat down. He did not do anything. What was there to do? Now, the Chief knew what he knew. Decisions would come from upstairs. He hoped.

The Governor was impressed by the Chief's report, and gave the order, "Take over."

Friendly was back in the Chief's office five minutes after the Governor had hung up.

He was ordered to proceed to Los Angeles the next day to investigate the circumstances surrounding the *L.A. Times* advertisement.

He was to contact the L.A. District Office, and organize a raid on all STAB's district headquarters in the Los Angeles area.

He hoped that he could get organized before the 'hens flew the coop.'

CHAPTER TWENTY-EIGHT

Upcountry, in Sebastopol, General Forrest Long was inspecting and re-inspecting his instruments of war.

Practically nothing had gone wrong. All deliveries had been made on time.

He had been concerned a week or so before, when an uninvited airplane had landed. He'd been able to dispatch the pilot and passenger with a minimum of information. Thank God the cannons hadn't been lying around waiting to be mounted. This work was now done, way under the trees, and heavily camouflaged.

At no time in the history of truck design and manufacture had a more puissant use been made of a simple delivery van.

The adapted trucks were provided with firing power on all sides and the roof: they were defensible from any direction.

The word 'defense' had not occurred to Forrest Long. He thought only in offensive terms.

Each van had the firepower of several Sherman tanks. Of course, the vehicles would not have won any prizes for cross-country maneuvers. However, such demands would not be made. Just easy sailing down Highway 101, south, and into position on the bridge.

Ten men plus two drivers would be assigned to each truck. These men were armory experts. Two other trucks were headquarters trucks. They carried the communication equipment, and some armament. Then there were the heavy-duty cannons which would control the main perimeter.

Long had made several foot trips across the bridge, spotting exactly where he wanted to deploy his vehicles. He had climbed the rugged terrain above the Marin tower. With proper placement of fire power, control could be assured during the time it took to mine the bridge.

One problem which could develop during the arrival involved traffic caught between the towers, after the trucks were in position. He figured that a six-minute clearing time would be needed.

A STAB detail, wearing simulated Highway Patrol uniforms, would direct what traffic there was past the barriers. In the excitement, compounded by red-and-white flashing lights, the absence of police cars would not be noted. However, for an official police car caught up in this net, there would be a harsher program.

The trucks would be moved into position at three a.m.

The time was set.

Very light traffic.

Maybe fog or wind and rain.

General Long worked out the sequence for closing the lanes. Finally, he decided to make the approach completely from the Marin side.

The first group of three vehicles would proceed across the bridge. The second group of three would reach the barrier point just past the Marin tower.

The group would wheel in such a way as to block all southbound lanes, and all but one of the northbound. All of this was worked-out using toy trucks as models.

As soon as the vehicles had stopped, flashing red-and-white lights would be activated. The traffic-control detail, with strong flashlights, would direct any southbound traffic into U-turns.

Two men would station themselves at the north-bound lane, to speed up any traffic caught between the two barriers. A man on a small motorcycle would follow the last car to the San Francisco barrier. The northbound lane would then be closed. Flares would mark a turnaround for southbound traffic approaching from the Marin side. Loudspeakers would order motorists to leave the bridge.

The problem at the San Francisco side would be handled somewhat differently.

Because of the proximity of bridge police, the vehicles would be wheeled into position on the landward side of the tower, ready for action.

Long figured that, on the San Francisco side, if there was any disruption of traffic, not more than three minutes could elapse before a tollgate complainant would trigger a general alarm. By that time, the vehicles should have command of the 'goddamned' beachhead.

Advancing police vehicles would be blasted to kingdom come. Too bad. But necessary.

As soon as the situation was secure, radio contact would be made with the Bridge Authority, the Army and the Coast Guard. Vandingan would make it clear that the bridge was seized, and would be completely destroyed, unless certain demands were met within 24 hours. Any attempt to come onto the bridge would be met with force.

Formal demands would be stated at 6:00 a.m.: "These matters will concern the Governor of the State of California and the Treasurer of the United States. Both of these officers should be alerted and prepared to act."

As soon as the barrier was placed, Wilton and his engineers would go to work. Their major task had to be completed before daylight: the explosives wired, and everything ready.

The standard operating procedure now called for a two hour and forty minute schedule. Twelve minutes had been added as a margin for error.

CHAPTER TWENTY-NINE

At the Reno airport, Puggo took delivery of the two Lear jets with the special take-off mechanisms. He and a company pilot flew them to Santa Rosa.

"Good luck," cried the Lear pilot, as he headed back to Reno in the company plane which had followed.

Puggo now took his plane over to Sebastopol and practiced landings. During one of the landings, he picked up Wilton and flew him to Santa Rosa. Wilton folded himself into 'his' plane. He and Puggo then put their planes through various intricate maneuvers.

They flew past the bridge several times, crossing it in the direction which would eventually take them all to the Marquesas.

It wasn't going to be easy, but it could be done.

The trick was to get the plane airborne and maneuverable within 2500 feet. It would have to take off to the south. By making a fast take-off, the plane could be off the 'runway' to a height of at least 200 feet. A light bank to the west, a little descent to pick up speed, then straight out the Golden Gate. And freedom.

Three heavy helicopters had been provided for the STAB group at Sebastopol. These would evacuate them from the bridge, plus three Army hostages, one for each helicopter. The automatic firing devices in the barricade would be activated to discourage intrusion onto the bridge before the group escaped.

Vandingan reorganized the landing points for his people. His pilots would hedge-hop to the landing areas. Fast ground transportation was being arranged. These fellows would disappear into the country as quickly as an egg yolk slides down the kitchen drain.

Orpath and Vandingan decided B-day would be the following Tuesday.

There would be a new moon, if it could be seen at all. The weather forecast promised clouds, with the possibility of a good storm.

So be it. The die was cast. Rubicon would be crossed.

As soon as personnel and equipment were moving, those left behind would break camp.

The Stinson Beach Seadrift group would move to Sebastopol after burning the working models and mechanisms which had become a part of their lives.

Toward the meeting's end, Vandingan, surrounded by his captains: Black, Forrest Long, and Wallace Shoppe, said, "Mr. Orpath, in these last moments of our project, we want you to know that we are highly appreciative of what this association can bring us, and we are grateful to you for giving us this opportunity."

Orpath, not expecting such a courteous compliment, was taken off-balance.

"Thank you," he croaked. "It's . . . ah, been an honor, ah, to know you too, and I should say that we appreciate *your* assistance. I hope that what we have contributed will serve your purposes."

George smiled at Vandingan and Black. Vandingan smiled back and thought to himself, "You damned little con man." Aloud he said, "It takes all types,

George, as can be seen from our association with this project."

Sunday. Everybody moved to Sebastopol.

Puggo took the team for a ride in the Lear. They practiced getting in and out. Their combined weight was scarcely a quarter of the rated payload, providing plenty of room for the goodies and the benefit of added speed. Take-offs from the Sebastopol runway were made within the 2500-foot limits.

They flew down past the bridge. To the extent that he could, Puggo simulated the maneuver that he'd have to go through to get off the bridge.

The plane wheeled, soared like a bucking horse. Jeri blessed her seat-belt.

Wilton took the controls. If the plane was damaged in take-off, he hoped that it could at least make it to Sebastopol, where they could change to the other plane. He landed the plane smoothly on the broad Sebastopol landing strip.

Orpath was very impressed, not only with the operation, but also with his choice of personnel.

Quarters at Sebastopol were crowded now, and not very comfortable. However, Shoppe had supplied a very good mess operation, and there were movies during the evening. One movie- supplier had amusingly included "The Bridge of St. Luis Rey."

Monday. Muscles tensed. The trucks were loaded. Ammunition was checked. K-ration-type food boxes were issued, and an extra supply loaded.

Puggo, who had a small communication shack near the runway, would be in constant touch with events. Both planes were at the ready. The trees some distance behind the shack acted as hanger space.

It would take about seventeen minutes to get into position on the bridge, once Puggo had the green light.

Pickup would be made at the Marin tower.

Departure time for the convoy was set for 1:00 a.m. Tuesday. There would be a midnight alert.

Until then, the team tried to get some sleep.

Orpath fell asleep like a child as soon as he'd had his dinner. Wilton was nervous. Jeri was excited. George resorted to gum-chewing.

Nothing was seen of Vandingan, although his lieutenants conferred here and there.

Finally, midnight.

The camp sprang alive.

Motors revved.

By 12:45, each person was in position.

Shoppe's assistants checked the personnel list for each van, then permitted each to enter.

At 1:00 a.m., the convoy began to move.

Onto Highway 101. No trouble. Then, a steady pace at 45 mph, with the vehicles spread over a mile.

On the Waldo Grade, the vehicles closed in.

By the time they approached the bridge, the weather was overcast and windy. Wisps of fog scudded through the bridge rigging.

Good.

Smaller demolition vehicles took the Fort Baker turn-off to Lime Point.

On the bridge, the first three trucks kept right on going toward the San Francisco tower.

There was one small station wagon in front of them. The lead truck's driver let it get away from him. Two cars passed, going in the opposite direction.

On the Marin side, the barrier formed. The two northbound cars slowed.

The 'police' waved them through.

A kid in a low-rider car spun southward. He saw the barrier, hit his brakes, skidded, hit the curb, and rolled onto the sidewalk. The 'police' approached the wreck. The driver was dead.

This eventuality had not been discussed. The 'police' chose to handle it like a 'refusal.'

They dumped the badly-broken body into the fog. The wreck extended the barrier.

White-and-red lights flashed. Glowing orange cones funneled traffic into the U-turns. A Mercedes slowed, hesitated, and turned.

On the San Francisco end, Long waved the first barrier truck into its position. The others followed. For nearly two minutes, absolutely no traffic.

The San Francisco mini-barrier was in place.

Two night-owls curved out from the toll plaza. Each concluded, in the murk, that some sort of bridge construction was going on.

They slowed down. A 'police officer' waved them into a U-turn. They obeyed reluctantly. The problem was made evident when each driver objected to the toll taker about having to pay for their aborted trip onto the bridge.

Three minutes passed. Then, a siren, and a flashing police light.

As the police car rounded the bend, an earsplitting explosion stopped it. A police officer jumped out and ran into the gloom like a scared rabbit. One more explosion and the police car was a small, flat mass of burning rubble. A warning.

Vandingan said into the radio, "Police! Hear this. The Golden Gate Bridge is closed to all traffic." He said it clearly, three times. The Highway Patrol responded, "We hear you. Move those trucks out of of the way. You're in violation of the Highway Code."

Vandingan again: "We will shortly be in violation of more than that. You'd better close all bridge approaches."

CHP radio, just then advised of what had happened to the squad car, could be heard putting out a May Day.

Traffic, stopped at the toll plaza, turned into the southbound lanes.

Lights went on around the toll plaza, as officers held a hasty conference.

No one suggested using another police car.

One man had crawled along the rail. When he'd gone as far as he could, he leaned over to see what he could.

The last thing he saw on earth was some blinking lights and a blue-red flash. He heard the beginning of an explosion.

His body was pulled back by a Highway Patrol buddy.

Vandingan again, loudly and clearly, announced, "We want EVERYONE behind the toll plaza."

Excited chatter broke into the police radio. Someone had not closed the microphone. "What the hell is this? . . . Don Wehrel was creamed! Who are these bastards? For crissake, close that microph . . ."

The night shift at the toll plaza had its hands full. The San Francisco police arrived. Highway Patrol was pushing its authority.

One newly-arrived police lieutenant jawed at a Highway Patrol officer, "OK, OK, you go to the Marin Tower and take over."

"Yeah," said the CHP type. "How do you suggest I get there?"

"Swim," snarled the lieutenant.

Orpath had now found Vandingan.

"We plan to have them on the horn at 6:00 a.m.," said Vandingan.

"Right," agreed a strained Orpath.

Vandingan opened his mike. "Now hear this. We will make a demand at 6:00 a.m. Have the Governor and the Secretary of the Treasury ready to speak. Any attempt to approach this bridge, from any direction, will be met with force."

He repeated this twice.

"Relax," he said quietly to Orpath.

Orpath left the communication area to find George.

George had taken a motorcycle to the Marin Tower, where Jeri was working. Everyone seemed busy at some appointed task. Wilton's first job had been to sabotage the bridge's lighting system. A well-placed crowbar shorted the power. It would be quite some time before the system could be restored.

A steadily-growing stream of cars from Marin had made the U-turn, with varying degrees of irritation, until the police on the Marin side had closed off the Waldo approach.

The more serious commuters had headed for the Richmond-San Rafael Bridge. The ferry would not start running until 6:30 a.m.

Long's observation point detail had taken over. All approach defenses were in place. He put this over the radio to Vandingan.

Wilton's plan worked. Within two hours, all cables were wired.

One crew worked at cutting through the floor of the bridge, under the San Francisco tower. Another worked at the Marin end. They'd need forty minutes to place the main load of dynamite.

The service road to Lime Point was ready to blow and land around the base of the Marin tower was being booby trapped.

Jeri helped finish setting up the Marin tower first-aid station. George offered her a ride back to the city side to set one up there, too. Dawn was just suggesting itself as they sailed along.

"Georgie," she yelled into his ear, "ain't nothing like it." And she squeezed him.

They were approaching a murky section of the bridge. George slowed his motorcycle and stopped,

Jeri's arms tight around his waist. He turned and kissed her. Slowly, they left the bike and found the bridge railing.

Jeri took George's head in her hands and looked at him deeply, as if drinking in, for some future memory, what she saw.

"Georgie," she whispered, "it all started just for fun. I love you Georgie. I shouldn't, but I do."

He kissed her and nuzzled into her ear, "OK Jeri."

"What's going to happen Georgie? Are we going to get out?"

"Yes. Yeah, sure." George looked into the nothingness around them. He hoped, but he wouldn't be sure until the plane cleared the railing in front of them.

There was a long moment of oneness. Then one sigh followed another. There was not another sound. Not one sound. They could hardly see each other, but they could feel.

"It's warm, Georgie. I don't understand. It's warm."

George looked at her and winked. "Earthquake weather," he said, turning back to the bike.

Tooling along, they waved to the engineers plying their destructive trade.

George pretended he was piloting the plane off the bridge. Just as he, in his mind's eye, was ready to pull up, he realized that he was driving past some light posts which must be forty feet high. These could cause a real problem for Puggo at takeoff.

Reaching the San Francisco tower, he went straight to Wilton and told him about the light posts.

Ed, miffed that he hadn't foreseen this danger, took a crew to cut them down.

Puggo would thank him later.

CHAPTER THIRTY

At 6:00 a.m., Vandingan manned his microphone.

"Are you through to the Governor?"

"We are."

"Mr. Governor?"

"Mr. Vandingan."

"How did you know?"

"Who else?"

"Mr. Governor, you have twenty hours to produce eleven members of STAB whom you are holding prisoner. We want these eleven men delivered to us at the Marin tower of the Golden Gate Bridge, with full pardons granted."

"Is that all?"

"No."

"What more?"

"Action — a word not always understood by the bureaucracy of this State. You understand it, though, and I assume you understand that people will be swimming back and forth without a bridge if we don't have those men by two a.m. tomorrow." He added, "Please tell your engineers that this bridge has been wired completely. If we are disappointed, it will just slide into the bay. Later on in the morning, at 10:00, our engineer will explain the wiring arrangements and the members affected. It will be an impressive recitation."

Vandingan handed his mike to Orpath.

Orpath's voice crackled. "Mr. Secretary of the Treasury, are you there?"

"This is Secretary Bronson."

"Good."

"Who the hell are you?"

"We may both be in hell when you find out."

A garbled sound came from the secretary.

"Now listen, Mr. Secretary, listen, and listen good. By two o'clock tomorrow morning you will deliver to the San Francisco tower the following: 2500 U.S. government bearer bonds in the $10,000 denomination, and $300,000 in unmarked fifties."

He added, "If we are satisfied with what you send us, you will have your bridge back."

Vandingan took the microphone. "Gentlemen, there is no negotiation. Just do as we have outlined, and don't try to come aboard until you bring us the goods."

A small explosion, followed by rapid fire from a heavy machine gun, interrupted.

Vandingan looked out. One of his men ran to him, saying, "A Coast Guard party tried to land on the tower. We've capsized their boat."

Vandingan went back on the air. "Now, look fellows," he said like a teacher, "we told you not to do that. Mr. Governor, Mr. Secretary, your people tried to land here and we have had to sink them. Please restrain these fellows. We are not here as murderers, except as you force us to defend ourselves. Over and out."

The Governor, without words for once, gasped an order to get the Secretary of the Treasury on his private telephone line.

"Mr. Secretary?" he queried. "What do you think?"

His question presupposed that the Secretary could.

"Don't worry, Mr. Governor. The troops at the Presidio are organizing an assault."

"With what?"

"I don't know with what, but I'm told that help is on the way."

"That man Vandingan is not a fool. He'll do exactly what he says. He'll leave us without the bridge."

"The U.S. government will not respond to blackmail."

"Well said. I'd like to say the same thing about the State of California."

"Say it."

"It's hard. Can you imagine what will happen once that bridge is gone?"

Secretary Bronson, also a Californian, said, "Yep. Weekends will be interrupted. No peacock feathers, no Seadrift, unless you can swim or sail there."

The Governor said, "What about the people from Kansas City who want to see Muir Woods?"

"Damned if I know, Mr. Governor."

"I'd fight this, except that I know these lads *mean* what they damn say."

"Is the Army there yet?"

For an answer, a heavy barrage of cannon fire came through the Governor's radio monitor.

"What the hell is that?"

"The Army must've arrived. Hang on." The Governor switched to the police line. "What was that?"

"The Army moved in some tanks."

"Good."

"Not good."

"Why?"

"Everyone of them was knocked out on the first whack."

"Goddamn."

"Yes, sir."

Back to Bronson. "It *was* the Army. They've run back down the hill to get some more tanks."

"Don't tell me!"

"I am telling you."

"Where's the Air Force?"

"That was considered, but scratched."

"Scratched! Why?"

"One stray salvo and we hit their dynamite system, and there goes your ball game."

"Guess that makes sense."

"Does the President know?"

"He's being told."

The Governor then said quietly, "Mr. Secretary, may I suggest that we pay these bastards off before they make idiots of us all? San Francisco is aware there is a problem now. In another hour the whole country will know, and by midafternoon, the whole world will be in on it."

The Secretary said, "So what?"

"Mr. Secretary, the Golden Gate Bridge may not mean very much to you and me, we're Californians, but to Americans all over the country it's a sentimental memory, a showplace; and to Europeans, it's a shrine."

"What are you suggesting?"

"I'm suggesting that we pay these people off. Get them off the bridge and then go after them. But get rid of them now, before we have a *real* problem."

"I hear you. I'll see how many of those $10,000 bonds we have. Lordy, Lordy! In the meantime, I suppose the President will fly off his rocker."

The Governor said goodbye, leaving the Secretary as close to tears as any Secretary of the Treasury has ever been, except, perhaps, Alexander Hamilton, as he saw Aaron Burr's bullet on the way to rip his waistcoat.

The Army and the Coast Guard not having been able to penetrate the bridge defenses, the Navy was brought into the picture.

On far-away Angel Island, the Navy brass was informed of the bridge dilemma. Certain high officers smiled broadly when they were told of the tank confrontation. But, being true servants of the Defense Department, they reefed these superior smiles and took seriously the potential problem which they could sense was looming before them.

High-rankers called for maps, plans, and low-rankers. A full dress conference took place, as a result of which the low-rankers took the plans, maps, etc. to their quarters with the orders to develop a plan for Naval participation.

The force was to be led by Captain Rodgers Bridgeman of Phoenix, Arizona. He had been a real cowboy prior to his appointment to Annapolis and his service as a marine commando.

At ten o'clock Wilton recited an impressive statement about the manner in which the bridge had been mined. The forces listening realized they were up against superior planning.

CHAPTER THIRTY-ONE

Dodds the Intrepid began the day checking truck movements. Heavy trucks would certainly be needed to carry such a load of armored-plate steel.

He went from gas station to gas station. He inquired of the California Highway Patrol. He drove the back country, hoping to run across the track marks of a heavy rig.

By accident, he talked to a shopkeeper in Sebastopol, who said that a big truck had stopped in front of his store "maybe two weeks ago." He remembered it because the vibrations from the engine shook up his shelves. As he had several tiers of cheap glassware for sale at high prices, he'd been worried. The truck driver had come in to ask directions to a certain cider mill, in the hills behind Sebastopol. The shopkeeper knew the place, because it had a big concrete runway, used during the War for practice landings. After the War, kids used it as a drag-strip. He had told the truck driver to look for an old cider sign beside the road.

Dodds' eyes popped, and he pulled the chain on the shopkeeper's reminiscences of youth. Dodds thought he knew where the cider mill was located. He'd passed such a sign on the back roads.

He rushed back to his car and drove toward the orchard area. He remembered the place the shopkeeper had described.

Where was that damned entrance! Around a little bend and down a dip in the road. Praise be! There it was, just as he had seen it earlier in his prowlings.

He drove in, trying to look just thirsty. He could find no one.

He drove around to the rear. He did find a quantity of garbage and a pile of other waste material, including some large pieces of cut metal waste. Aha!

He was in the right place.

He drove further, and finally came upon the landing strip. In front of him was a dilapidated shack. He knocked on the door.

Puggo turned off his receiver and answered the door.

Dodds, following FBI instructions, flipped open his identification.

Puggo nearly had a heart attack.

Collecting himself, he squeaked, "What do you want?"

Dodds described, in Jack Webb-FBI, a tally of what the infringements had been.

"Look, Mister," whined Puggo, "I'm just a watchman here."

"Who was doing the metal-work?"

"Oh, them. They left."

"When?"

"Days ago."

"What were they doing?"

"Building racing cars."

"Racing cars? Out of armored steel?"

"Well, these were the kind you put in a field, and then they all bang into each other."

"Yeah?" from Dodds.

"Yeah," from Puggo.

"Where did they go?"

"Sacamenna, I think. County Fair Grounds."

Dodds was smug. "County Fair in March?"

"No, they just use the grounds there."

"Oh."

Dodds set out for "Sacamenna." He returned to Highway 101 and proceeded south. As he was driving along, he clicked on his radio.

". . . Bridge has been barricaded . . . held for ransom. Here is Ruth Joyner, in a helicopter, with an eyewitness report."

"The barricades are big moving vans. They evidently are armed. One CHP car has been attacked and blown up. A Coast Guard boat has capsized. Six Army tanks are disabled at the San Francisco toll plaza. These people know what they want, and they've threatened to blow up the bridge unless they get it."

And so on, into Dodds' ears and mental processes. Finally he put two and two together. Those vans. They were armed. If they were armed, then they must also have armor protection.

Armor-plate steel!

Violation of Section B-149-A. No yellow copy!

He sped forward.

In his mind, Dodds had the culprits cornered on the Golden Gate Bridge.

CHAPTER THIRTY-TWO

Fifteen minutes after it was broadcast from the bridge, the May Day reached the night-duty officer at Sacramento FBI District Headquarters.

He immediately called his Chief, who asked to be put through to Friendly in L.A.

A drowsy Friendly answered an insistent telephone.

"Ben?"

"Yeah . . . oh, uh, hello, Chief."

"Sorry, but it's hit the fan."

"What's that?"

"Vandingan and his crew have just taken the Golden Gate Bridge!"

"Well, well, well."

"Get here, pronto."

"Yes, Sir."

"I'll meet you at the toll plaza."

"I'm on my way."

They met a little before ten, just as Wilton began his discription. The place looked like a battlefield. It was.

The frustrated CHP and San Francisco police were still at each others' throats over strategy.

The Chief and Friendly became observers. The first, and saddest, thing Friendly observed was the barricade. He recognized the vans which were supposed to be hauling waste at San Onofre!

Someone had gone too far. Others had not gone far enough.

The day was otherwise blooming beautifully. No wind, lots of sun. Very dry. You could see swallows on Alcatraz.

A number of airplanes were now overhead, and the ack-ack was on alert. Just in time, too.

An Air Force plane came over. Received a warning shot. It came over again, and received a full load just behind the left wing. The plane veered and exploded as it hit the water. The pilot had ejected in a matter of seconds.

To some older hands, who had seen aircraft-carrier service, it was like old times.

At noon, Vandingan again called the Governor and the Secretary of the Treasury.

"How are we coming?"

"Progress," said the Governor.

"The President wants to talk to you," accused the Secretary of the Treasury.

"Here I am," said Vandingan.

"What the hell y'aul trine tah do, Boy?" came over the loudspeakers.

"Mr. President."

Not hearing, the President said, "This is yar Preseydent, Boy."

"Yes, Sir," said Vandingan.

"Get the hell off'n that bridge!"

"The Governor knows when that will happen, and so does your Secretary of the Treasury."

"You trine to stomp on me, Boy?"

"No, Sir. Just get us our people and the money, and we'll go home."

"Y'ull go to jail, that's where y'ull go."

"Please don't yell so loud. This dynamite is tricky stuff."

"Dynamite? Boy, what are ya fixin' tah do?"

"Mr. Secretary, you tell him. Also tell him that if he doesn't let you act quickly, the French are going to laugh at us again. We wouldn't want that, would we?"

"No," sobbed the Secretary.

"Over and out."

Underneath the bridge, as if it would never fall, many pleasure craft were being shooed away by a very careful Coast Guard cutter.

Airplanes and police helicopters kept their distance. The Army was awaiting the outcome of a staff meeting. Navy low rankers were calculating the distance between the bridge's understructure and the crow's nest of the Enterprise at the moment before that particular high tide would change direction.

CHAPTER THIRTY-THREE

Dodds' gas pedal hit the floor.

Zipping around slower-moving traffic in the vicinity of the Marin Civic Center, he was intercepted by a fast-moving patrol car.

Displaying his ID, he explained his mission. The police officer, aware of the bridge problem, said, "Follow me!" And away they went at high, and even terrifying, speed.

As they approached the police roadblock at the Sausalito turnoff, the CHP pulled his car over, and the officer suggested that Dodds proceed in the police car. Dodds jumped in.

Shortly after they passed the Stinson Beach turnoff, heading for the bridge, they saw a police command unit. They stopped and conferred. They were informed they could not proceed further. Dodds was furious.

He almost screamed that he had to serve papers on the ones who owned the trucks.

The police laughed.

Dodds was shaking.

All of a sudden, a TV monitor picked up a great scurrying-around on the bridge.

The Army had made its move: gas. They dumped it to the west and depended on the wind to carry it across the bridge.

Vandingan's people were alerted, and were under their gas masks before it hit. The prevailing four o'clock wind blew it right past the bridge and south, but not before it had knocked out ninety percent of the bridge police and administrative people. That is, on the San Francisco side.

Very strong, that gas.

Three Army mess halls were contaminated, as well as the posh St. Francis Yacht Club, and a large number of dwellings in the Marina District. So much for Army intervention.

When the gas hit, Friendly and his Chief were in a small office in the Administrative Building. They were not affected.

An intercom warned them of the danger. Since the Chief had brought along riot equipment from Sacramento, they could equip themselves with gas masks, which was more than most of the personnel at the toll plaza could do.

Friendly wondered if he could take advantage of the diversion to get through the barricade. He'd been told of the shooting of Officer Wehrel. The Chief abandoned the idea. What could be done there, anyway?

So they just watched.

Ambulances arrived to speed away the gas-contaminated employees.

As the sun disappeared, two things happened. The Navy gave itself the go-ahead on their plans to seize the bridge and the Governor capitulated. So excited by the prospects in two different directions were the participants, that neither communicated with the other.

Informed that the prisoners and their pardons would be delivered as requested, Jeri smiled, "Isn't that nice of the Governor, and him not running for re-election or anything."

Serious young Navy personnel with marine commando background began putting together the materiel for the Navy assault.

At 6:30, General Forrest Long doubled his guard by bringing in most of his mountain boys.

Finally, around ten, word came from the Secretary of the Treasury: national policy had been made to save the bridge. For the moment, in the name of national unity, the requirements would be met.

Effort was being made right then to schedule delivery of money and prisoners.

The Army would supply three officers as hostages to accompany the STAB helicopters. The Aide-de-Camp of the Commanding General was to be one of these officers. The Post Commander and the Special Services Officer would complete the troops.

Vandingan said that, for convenience these officers could report to the San Francisco tower.

Everything was working very well. Puggo had been contacted and given an approximate departure time.

In the gloom and calm of night, at slack tide, the Navy undertook its daring program to get their personnel onto the bridge. The great aircraft carrier had previously been scheduled to leave port at 2200 hours, because for such a large ship the slack tide makes for better control, particularly where there is no wind.

Normally there is no watch posted on the high mast, but this particular departure was delayed for some unusual activity in this particular crow's nest. Sailors carried breeches-buoy equipment up the steep ladders. This odd-shaped arrangement was followed by coils of rope. Each sailor carried one coil looped over each shoulder. Six such coils were delivered to the crow's nest.

When these preparations had been made, two officers and Captain Bridgeman, in a wet suit, ascended into the nest. They tested the equipment and assured themselves that they had what they needed.

In this equipment was included a small Lyle gun used for shooting line.

The men withdrew to the board room. There, spread upon the table, were the detailed blueprints of the central part of the bridge span.

The men studied them; particularly the profile of the beams. They saw that a well-aimed Lyle projectile could carry with it a lead rope which would clear the first beam and return to the deck.

When the heavier rope was attached to the lead rope, it would be hoisted into place and returned to receive a breeches-buoy.

The ship would have to be closely controlled to permit the accomplishment of this difficult procedure. The crew needed stability for about forty seconds. The procedures had been timed for thirty-two seconds.

Once the breeches-buoy was in position, Captain Bridgeman could be pulled up to the beam level where he could establish a 'beach-head' under the bridge. He would secure the six lines and drop them, one after the other, back to the carrier's deck where they would fall into the hands of the six wet-suited commandos whom Bridgeman had chosen for the detail. These men would then climb the ropes to the beam level from which Bridgeman was operating. Their assignment, once they gained the bridge floor, was to defuse as much of the dynamite as they could.

It was hoped that if their presence was spotted, a diversion would be created during which the police and Army personnel could take the barricades.

The large ship slid from its berth across the dark and placid water of the Bay, just at the moment when

Nature's tidal forces paused. No lights, no noise, just a great silent hulk moving slowly toward the sea.

Eyes strained to seek the shadow of the span. Without warning, a great black wing swept out of the darkness. Mast and shadow met. The ship shuddered to a stop. Hands, arms, ropes, buoy, Lyle gun all performed in the planned pattern. The end of the Lyle gun's missive, made visible by phosphorescent tape, returned to the deck to be attached to the heavier rope. Within seconds, the loop was made and Bridgeman in his wet suit and with his heavy load was being pulled into the air toward the supporting grill of the bridge.

The ship sustained its position long enough for him to make contact with his perch on the beam. Fortunately, the lead rope had passed over an upper beam so that Bridgeman was able to operate with far more ease than if he had had to approach the ledge from below.

He worked feverishly attaching the lines which were to drop to the carrier's deck. Eager hands seized the ropes as they dropped. The rest of his assault personnel crawled to the beam. They huddled like birds on a telephone wire.

As Wilton and the rest had not anticipated any approach to this part of the bridge's underbelly, no electronic warning devices had been placed.

Surprised and pleased that the weather and the tide had permitted so much to be accomplished so quickly, the Captain gave the signal for the great ship to proceed. Its black bulk slowly disappeared under the commando experts, each of whom attached himself to a strong safety rope which had been one of this team's first installations.

Each man sought his prearranged position to climb to the bridge deck.

When Dodds heard that the government had caved in, he was outraged. His government. "The FBI would pursue to the death."

Here, Dodds was the man on the spot. Why not increase *his* authority? He could arrest all of them.

Dodds, of course, was not realistic. He asked that his mission be communicated to the Commander.

It was, by radio, to General Forrest Long.

"Who the hell is this?" cried Forrest, without embellishment.

"I am from the FBI, Sir," said Dodds into a little microphone. "I have papers in my hand to serve upon your employer."

"My employer?"

"Yes. Your employer is in contravention of Section B-149A, relative to your armor-plate. You do have armor-plate, don't you?"

"Oh, yes, and armor too," smirked Forrest Long.

"I have not been given authority to apprehend you for armor. Now, about this armor-plate . . ."

A mild explosion signalled an attempt by frogmen to approach the Marin pylon base. Sporadic machine-gun fire was picked up through the radio speakers.

Dodds was shocked. Firing at the FBI! Somebody would answer for that!

"The armor-plate . . ." he stammered on a second try.

"What about it?" said Forrest.

"Your use of it is without appropriate authority, that's 'what about it'!" Dodds shrieked into his microphone.

Dodds was losing control. It was dark and it was cold. He was dressed for a warm day in Sebastopol. He looked like a hunted fox.

He moved away from the microphone. He surveyed

the TV screen and the Richardson grade. Then, he began to run into the gloom.

He was in good shape. He loped along the highway, through the tunnel, around the curve and onto what he dimly recognized as the bridge. Before he knew it, he was facing the barricade.

He slowed down. Just as he did, a searchlight found him. A loudspeaker blasted the voice of Forrest Long. "Hold it, boy. Advance with your hands up."

Dodds stopped in his tracks. Nature whispered to him to do what the nice man said.

He did. He walked forward. Slowly.

Right in front of him, an arm motioned to him from what seemed like a solid barrier. He followed the suggestion.

Never was one FBI agent so quickly handcuffed as young Mr. Dodds. Not only his hands, but also his feet.

He was pushed into the glowering presence of General Forrest Long.

"Now, what the hell do *you* want?"

"I am Agent Dodds, FBI, and I am here to serve you papers for not properly completing your permit application in connecion with Form B-149A, necessary for all purchase of armor-plate."

All Long could say was, "Well, I never! Put this s.o.b. in the guard truck, and tie him down."

Handcuffed inside, Dodds carefully scrutinized his surroundings. Sure enough! Armor-steel plate everywhere. He had caught these fellows with the goods!

Commando Bridgeman chose to move toward the San Francisco tower. There was enough activity overhead to discourage the immediate entry on to the bridge to cut the dynamite connections. He pulled himself onto the safety beam, and waited.

CHAPTER THIRTY-FOUR

At 11:30, the radio signaled. Vandingan was on. "What is it?"

"The Treasury people are here," the operator said.

"Where are the Army people?"

"Here and ready."

"I'll get right back to you." Vandingan relayed the news to his lieutenants who informed Wilton.

Fortunately, the FBI was better-represented on the San Francisco side by Friendly than by Dodds on the Marin side.

Friendly listened to the discussion of money and hostages. His computer was going to work full blast. He went right to the place where these officers waited: the front office, overlooking the toll booths.

The General's Aide was a good-sized man. The Post Commander was skinny. But the Special Services Officer was just right. He was a rumpled man, slightly shorter than Friendly.

"Gentlemen," Friendly began. "I am FBI Agent Friendly." He showed them his badge.

"I have an idea," he continued, "which will permit me to infiltrate the STAB lines here."

The Post Commander bristled a little. He was a bird Colonel.

"Now, look here, Agent Friendly. We are here to act as hostages, not to get into any action. I will not permit these officers to endanger their lives, except as we have been ordered."

"Relax, Colonel," smiled Friendly. "One of you is going to be relieved of your assignment, namely, this pleasant officer, who is going to exchange clothing with me so that the FBI can pursue its duties if a conflict is involved."

The Colonel's mouth opened. But he didn't say anything. The Special Services Officer whom Friendly had singled out grinned. Friendly quickly checked his plan out with his Chief, who, on instant consideration, found it better than nothing.

The Special Services Officer looked a little over-dressed in Friendly's clothes. Friendly looked a little on the tight side in the officer's uniform.

But it would work.

Friendly was now in a position to go too far.

The Chief had already gone as far as he could go. He was busy trying to make liaison with the San Francisco Bureau of the FBI. Government property had been destroyed right in front of the Chief, and he was now ready to go to bat.

Friendly's job, as the disguised officer, was to upset the apple cart from inside, if he could. It was the only way to make up for his terrible failure to recognize trouble in Sebastopol. He was motivated.

The call came that the eleven STAB prisoners were at the Marin side.

The men were given safe conduct to the bridge by the police who withdrew immediately. The returned prisoners were told to walk down to the barrier. A happy welcome for old friends greeted them.

"We are glad to have you aboard," said Vandingan over the radio connecting him with the Marin barricade.

Vandingan asked that all the pardons be sent down

to him. He looked them over, saw that they were in order, and sent them back.

"We are nearly done," Vandingan announced to Orpath and George. "We'll get the money now. You check it. I'll give the order for the helicopters. Two on the Marin side, one on the San Francisco side. But we'll still control from here.

The money and the bonds were lugged from the toll plaza by the two officers and Friendly, in disguise. It went directly to Orpath's van.

The Post Commander and the General's Aide were ushered to the Marin tower. Friendly was to stay on the San Francisco side.

Orpath and his team began to count. The truck interior was well-lit.

Orpath, with the face of a lynx, riffled and checked. So did George. Jeri was helpful. The job was completed.

Wilton went to the radio room to contact Puggo in code. He told him that landing lights were arranged.

The team then was loaded, money and all, into a truck, and after hasty goodbyes to all at the San Francisco barrier, proceeded carefully to the Marin side to await Puggo.

It was nearly 2:00 a.m. There was no conversation. Each person was completely involved in his assigned duty.

Two of Vandingan's soldiers stood near Friendly. He looked around. The barricade was solid. The artillery was manned by four teams of alert gunmen.

For a moment, he thought that he could disarm one of his guards and use the weapon to wipe out one of the gunnery teams. If he was lucky, he might get the second group.

But to what advantage?

He could see why the Army was holding its fire. Every cable had its explosive message neatly-taped in position. One unfortunate shot, and the string of fireworks would start off, effecting the unthinkable.

"What the hell can I do?" he thought.

He called over to one of his guards. The man turned and asked what he wanted.

"I need to relieve myself," Friendly said nervously. "So?"

"May I go to the edge of the roadway?"

"You may not," snapped the guard. "Just stand where you are."

Friendly was cornered. What man could perform to his personal relief under such stress?

"The hell with it," he said.

The guard turned away for one instant. Friendly leaped from the ground, hit the guard a heavy blow behind the ear, and grabbed his machine-gun. The guard went down. His comrade began to level his gun.

Friendly shot it out of his hand. He knew he had only a moment. He turned his weapon to the barricade and loosed three bursts, which latticed the woodwork of the van. He hoped that some of them would penetrate.

Of course, none of his bullets had any effect, except to scratch the armor-plate behind the shattered woodwork.

Suddenly, with a shock, his elbow and hand went numb. The machine-gun he held clattered to the bridge floor. The pain he suffered was excruciating. Clutching his injured arm, he fell to his knees and then forward on his face.

"Won't this be a story to tell — shot in the funny bone," and he passed out.

169

It was, as they say, a nice try. Having made the physical effort to rectify his failure at Sebastopol, Friendly would feel better.

He had certainly risked his life.

When Bridgeman heard the machine-gun fire, he pulled himself level with the floor of the bridge so that he could see the drama and valiant defeat of Benjamin Franklin Friendly unfold before him.

He was making a decision to spring forward to take up Friendly's fight when the bridge burst into light and he was conscious of the noise of jet engines overhead. Wilton's landing-strip lights had been activated.

Suddenly, not fifty feet above him, a great jet bird rushed past.

Puggo was landing on schedule at 3:15.

He had cleared the World War II gun emplacements by 100 feet, and zeroed right in through the arch of the San Francisco pylon. He was fifty feet over the barrier. He touched down and taxied away in the direction of the Marin tower.

As Bridgeman cursed the fact that his walkie-talkie reception was made impossible by the steel girders of the bridge, a large helicopter arrived. At the same moment, two more had landed at the Marin tower which, of course, Bridgeman could not see.

In the early morning murk all of this hasty activity on the San Francisco pylon was obscured from all but Bridgeman, who found the speed of events confusing. He could conclude, however, that either reinforcements were arriving or that the invaders were leaving.

In the latter conclusion he would be correct.

Vandingan gave the order to board the helicopters. Friendly, under guard and handcuffed, was pushed into the waiting helicopter at the San Francisco tower. Everything was ready for the quick departure.

At the Marin tower, with Puggo's direction, STAB personnel helped load the Lear's cabin. Money, food, and light baggage. The team entered as they had practiced. Not one second lost.

Everyone belted in: Orpath with no expression; George, chewing and smiling at the same time; Wilton skeptical; Jeri with fingers crossed.

The middle barrier van moved to the curb, providing width for an extension of the runway for Puggo. He took his plane through this wide new channel and turned the plane so that it headed south. His engines roared until the Lear shook on its brakes.

With a great rush of power, they sped between the two remaining vans. Tensely, Wilton watched the descending hoop, to which the mined bridge cables were attached. At the right moment, he'd signal Puggo to pull up and wheel out. If he made one false move . . one fraction-of-a-second late . . .

He gave the signal. Up went the Lear, straight into the air.

Not straight. It wheeled heavily to the west.

It was clear of the bridge!

"Lucky we cut down the light posts," Wilton thought.

Nose down, speed up, and then, straight out of the Golden Gate, and into the grey of a new day.

CHAPTER THIRTY-FIVE

When the Lear cleared the bridge, the helicopters on the Marin side revved, as a wet dawn was breaking. As the commander of each barricade-vehicle left his post, he activated his automatic firing device. This started a barrage of tracer bullets north along the floor of the bridge, toward Marin. There were no takers for the pursuit.

Everyone ran to the helicopters, mounted, found a seat, and buckled in. Within seconds, the doors slammed shut. The Marin group was off. The remainder of the mountain group was being picked up in a similar manner.

At the San Francisco tower, after a sweeping look to be sure all were aboard, Vandingan crawled into his roaring helicopter.

His seat faced Friendly, handcuffed, and in great pain.

Benjamin Franklin Friendly immediately recognized Lauris Vandingan.

Erect, calm, handsome, unruffled, in control, and even pleasant. The trace of the smile was still on Vandingan's face. He looked across at Friendly. The smile broadened.

"FBI," he made himself heard over the helicopter's noise. "You are number two."

Friendly did not smile. He shrugged. He wondered what 'number two' meant.

He and Dodds, of course, had never met. Neither knew the other existed. Both were victims of what Vandingan was trying to abolish.

Bridgeman, helpless, watched the ascent of the great helicopter. Barricade commanders had activated the barricade guns to spray the bridge floor toward the toll plaza; being tracer bullets, the course they took was very visible.

Although he was not an ordnance man, Captain Bridgeman realized that if he could reach the gun emplacements he could de-activate the firing. He sprang forward, reaching the barricade just as the whole bridge seemed to buck like one of his Arizona broncos.

Vandigan, looking out the window as the helicopter rose into the air, wondered what the Army would do with the armored trucks.

He was attracted by what he thought were sparks. No, a giant string of firecrackers.

Horrified, he realized that what he saw was a series of explosions.

Explosions!

He riveted himself to the window. His vision of the Marin tower, right in front of him, seemed to lurch. He thought the helicopter's angle had changed. That it may have done, but the great tower continued its slow collapse until it slipped below the now sparkling waters of the Golden Gate.

Illuminated by the explosions, forms could be seen running and falling down. A landslide started by the highway.

"My God!" gasped Vandingan. "That wasn't in the deal!"

CHAPTER THIRTY-SIX

Vandingan did not find out what had happened until the radio blared it later.

At the moment the helicopters lifted, an 8.2 earthquake shook the Bay Area, along with most of Northern California.

There would be arguments until the end of time over which came first, the shake or the explosion.

It seemed as though some Superior Being was teaching a lesson in appreciation — the hard way.

Dodds, his search warrant, and the armor-plate vanished along with the Marin tower. Captain Bridgeman, performing an act of great valor, silenced the San Francisco barricade barrage. When he reached the toll plaza nothing was standing and bedlam reigned amongst those who could still walk. Of his six commandos, he accounted for only two.

Benjamin Franklin Friendly was more fortunate. His helicopter swooped along the coast, descending just long enough to deposit a relieved Special Agent on the sands of Stinson Beach.

The last thing Vandingan saw of Friendly was his smiling black face, as he watched the helicopter climb and head north to destiny.

The Lear purred its way to Puerto Vallarta.

The shock of the earthquake had diverted immediate attention of those who would otherwise pursue. Both San Francisco Airport and Alameda were in shambles. Hamilton Field, on the alert, sustained serious runway damage, and its communications had been interrupted at the crucial moment.

By the time services were restored, the Army, Navy, and Air Force faced more vitally-important problems than the pursuit of some petty crooks.

The Armed Forces were all switched into their natural-disaster disciplines.

Orpath and Vandingan were forgotten for the time.

Puggo, not realizing at first that there was no pursuit, flew low so that radar could not track the plane. He ran a parallel course about 500 miles off the coast.

Next day, refueled, they took off again for the Marquesas. Wilton was a competent co-pilot.

Four hundred miles short of their destination, it happened. They ran into a heavy headwind; and Puggo found a small leak in one of the fuel lines. The fuel line was closed, with a resulting loss of speed.

The fuel supply was just enough to carry them to the Marquesas. The fuel gauge was not encouraging.

"What the hell have you done wrong now?" snarled Wilton.

Puggo looked worried, and began considering alternate landing positions.

He studied the map.

The map showed only water between where he thought they were and where they wanted to be.

Puggo glanced out the window.

A speck.

He began to sweat.

He aimed at the speck.

As it came more into view, it looked quite clear. He circled.

He passed over the island. No landing strip, but

he saw that he could make a landing on what appeared to be pulverized coral.

He tried to find the wind.

With the tank's last cupful of fuel, he landed.

He said quietly, "We're down."

Orpath asked, "Where?"

Jeri muttered, "If this is the Marquesas, take me back to Utica!"

George stopped chewing his gum.

Wilton's face, for once, said it all. "*Anywhere* else!"

George opened the cabin door on desolation. One by one, they climbed out.

All but Puggo.

In the near distance, they spotted a large, weather-beaten sign, but could not read it. They wandered closer. As they came nearer, the painted words spelled:

RADIOACTIVE WASTE SATURATION:
USE COMPLETE SURVIVAL GEAR!

Puggo saw it through his field glasses.

Quietly, he closed the cabin door.

He switched to the reserve tank, started the motor, waved 'goodbye,' and took off, dumping his white coat out of the pilot's window.

There are some compensations for being odd-looking, and having an odd voice, and having an odd laugh.

With the wealth aboard that little airplane, Elton Puggo Alexander was over-compensated.

The End

NOTES

NOTES

NOTES

NOTES

NOTES

NOTES

NOTES

NOTES